nothing
to lose

Praise for
Kim Suhr

"Kim Suhr's *Nothing to Lose* is the kind of book I want when I scan a bookstore looking for an alluring surprise. Here are stories with heart and muscle, brilliantly imagined turns: A man is drawn into dark mischief with the night goggles he brought home from Iraq; a woman struggles to bury her son's pusher in the snow. Suhr's is the kind of voice that makes me feel held in the storyteller's hand."
—Steven Huff, author of *Blissful and Other Stories*

"Kim Suhr's *Nothing to Lose* will delight readers as it draws them in with the kindness, love, dogged determination, and steadfast hope embodied in these characters found throughout the towns and countrysides of Midwestern communities."
—Ann Angel, author of *Janis Joplin: Rise Up Singing*
2011 YALSA Award Winner

"Dialed-up like a high-tension wire buzzing down the middle of county road M outside of Waupun, Kim Suhr's new collection of stories is haunting, wise, and humane. She tells these tales with a pitch-perfect knowing voice, placing everyday loneliness, loss, and possibility in sharp, sometimes dangerous, focus. Suhr writes with whipsaw precision."
—Barry Wightman, author of *Pepperland*

nothing
to lose

Stories by
Kim Suhr

Cornerstone Press
Stevens Point, Wisconsin

Cornerstone Press, Stevens Point, Wisconsin 54481
www.uwsp.edu/cornerstone

Printed in the United States of America by:
Worzalla Publishing, Stevens Point, Wisconsin 54481

Library of Congress Control Number: 2018961314
ISBN: 978-0-9846739-7-1

Gratefully acknowledged are the following magazines:

"How to Play with Fire" originally published as "Play With Fire" in *Midwest Review*.
"How to Play with Fire" originally aired on *The Others Stories* podcast.
"Night Vision" originally published in *Solstice Literary Magazine*.
"Nothing to Lose" originally published in *Stonecoast Review*.
"Demise" originally published in *Fictive Dream*.
"Our Hoyles" originally published in *Literally Stories*.
"Deer Camp" originally published in *Full of Crow Fiction*.
"Brush Strokes" originally published in *Pink Panther Magazine*.

Cornerstone Press titles are produced in courses and internships offered by the Department of English at the University of Wisconsin–Stevens Point.

DIRECTOR & PUBLISHER-IN-CHIEF
Dr. Ross K. Tangedal

FALL 2018 STAFF
Madeline Swanger, Katy Nachampassak, Monica Swinick, Ashley Nickel, Michaela Bargender, Madeline Krueger, Grace Tesch, Lindsey Bundgaard, Sierra Willfahrt, Amanda Greenthal, Issadore McCusker, Elizabeth Lindloff, Elizabeth Strobel, Kellie Thiele, Emmalea Stirn, Brittany Kelly-Dillow, Rachel Zach, Paige Roy, Jacoby Schroeder, Breanna Camalieri, Kyle Beattie, Alexis Hoffman, Angela Stoker, Chris Dax

SENIOR PRESS ASSISTANTS
Caleb Baeten, Richard Wilkosz

For Rob

Contents

Night Vision 1

Our Hoyles 17

Justice 23

Right Place, Right Time 43

Deer Camp 57

How to Play with Fire 61

Open Book 73

Good News 89

To Understand 99

Demise 109

You Can't Win If You Don't Enter 119

For Your Service 131

Brush Strokes 143

Dry Spell 161

How We Got Our Baby 179

Nothing to Lose 205

Night Vision

Brad hadn't slept more than a few hours at a stretch since he'd dropped his duffle in the entryway of his grandfather's house and started his period of "reintegration." With the old man in rehab for a broken hip, Brad could sit in the plaid recliner for hours at a time watching war coverage on TV, smoking cigarettes, and catching a few winks here and there. From the recliner, he could see the doorway to the guest room where he was meant to sleep, but so far, the bed remained unused.

One night during his third week back in Madison, the sound of mortar fire blasted him awake. Brad found himself standing in the middle of the living room, searching frantically for his weapon, trying to figure out which direction the rounds had come from.

The TV. They were showing airstrikes on TV.

He shook his head to try to clear the pounding in his ears. "I gotta get outta here," he said aloud, his hands shaking.

He fished in the bottom of the duffle and grabbed his night vision goggles. "Let's see what you have to show me." He turned off the light, flicked off the TV, secured the goggles to his head and stepped outside.

The street was quiet, the traffic light on Regent Street already blinking red.

He found an old oak tree across from *Jingles'* with a clear view of the door, everything rendered in green and black tones. Two laughing women and a wobbly man stumbled out accompanied by a song Brad vaguely remembered. The three folded themselves into the front seat of the Cutlass and pulled out. He watched the car until it was out of sight.

Starting to take off the goggles, he heard music again and stopped—*Us and Them* by Pink Floyd—and he saw a woman, alone. Instead of getting into a car, she turned onto the sidewalk. She was going to walk home alone past midnight? Didn't she *know* what could happen to a long-haired woman alone in the dark?

He slowly descended the hill taking care to keep a safe distance and removed the goggles. He didn't want to scare the woman, just see her home safely. He kept a three- block distance, hidden in the shadows. Turning onto Vilas Avenue, she tripped on the sidewalk, and he almost sprinted to catch her. But she righted herself and took off her tippy sandals. Drunk.

She hooked the straps over her finger and continued walking. Without the shoes, she was sure-footed like someone who had spent a lot of time barefoot. Her toes pointed outward, she leaned into each step like a dancer. Not drunk at all.

She turned up the walk to a two-flat, fiddled with her key, and let herself into the first floor apartment. A wave of relief washed through Brad. She was home.

He walked across the street, sat on the curb in front of a parked car, and lit a cigarette. He watched her silhouette leave the front room, return, and douse the light. A car turned the corner illuminating the street. He considered moving on, but the parked car next to him cast a shadow. No one knew he was there. He could stay a while longer.

Crushing out the stub of his cigarette with his boot, he lit another and took a long, deep drag. He waited a half-hour, put on his goggles and gave her house one last sweep. No one hiding in the bushes. The door locked up tight. Or was it? He looked again. Her keys dangled from the lock. Although he figured no one would happen by and let himself into her house, Brad couldn't be sure.

He headed across the street planning to take the keys out of the lock, slip them onto an entryway table and pull the door closed, locking himself—and anyone else—out. But when he opened the door, he realized there was no way to lock it without setting the deadbolt from inside. The latch made a deafening click. He froze listening for a sign that she had heard him, that she was awake and coming to find him there in her entryway.

Afraid. Exposed.

Nothing.

He turned the deadbolt and crept toward the back of the house, passing the open door of her bedroom. He hadn't meant to stop. Knew he should keep going, get the hell out of there. But his gaze landed on her sleeping face, relaxed and untroubled. She lay on her side facing the door, her cheek slightly smooshed, making her lips ruffle. They looked like they wanted to give him a kiss.

She could be in so much danger, he thought. If I wanted to, I could snap her neck before she could open her eyes. He looked at his hands and thought of all the destructive things they had been taught to do, all the things he could do to her.

But she sleeps, he thought. She just . . . sleeps.

He watched the rise and fall of her chest beneath the covers, his breath falling into her rhythm. In. Out. In. Out. They breathed together. He closed his eyes. A bobber on a tranquil lake, he floated. No need to struggle. The calm nearly lulled him to sleep where he stood.

Then, his military training kicked in. Time to go.

The cadence of her breathing remained unbroken. Brad looked down and noticed the keys still clenched in his fist. Quietly, he set them on the dining room table and walked through the kitchen to let himself out.

Next morning, Brad woke up in his grandfather's ratty recliner. The remote sat on his lap where he had left it. He knew he should turn on something besides CNN, but every time his thumb moved toward the channel button, he thought of Zach and Abe, Duwan and Jeremy still sitting their asses in Iraq. Still getting shot at by crazy hajis. He couldn't change the channel or turn off the TV. Watching war coverage made him feel like he was walking the perimeter, keeping them safe. It was the least he could do after getting discharged early and abandoning them.

Most guys would have celebrated the chance to get the hell out of there with their asses intact, but Brad's discharge had been less-than-honorable and less-than-celebratory. On the day of his dismissal, he had answered the requisite questions and signed the requisite forms. When it came time to inventory his military-issue items, the sergeant noticed his night vision goggles were missing. Brad told him they had been lost in his final mission, saying the word "mission" with a hint of sarcasm. A look of brittle understanding crossed the sergeant's face. He handed Brad a blank Material Loss Report Form and left the room without a word. The sooner Private Williams blended back into civilian life the better, as far as the Army was concerned.

Why Brad had kept his night vision goggles, he couldn't say. He had simply slid them into the bottom of his duffle and packed his few other belongings on top.

He knew he should put the goggles back into the bag and leave them there, but each night for the next week, his thoughts returned to the woman and the peace he had felt while watching her sleep. A peace he hadn't felt since long before Iraq. More importantly, he had made sure she'd gotten home safely and her doors were locked up tight. He thought of other women who, right at that moment, needed his protective eye watching over them. Maybe that was why he had kept the goggles in the first place—to shield defenseless women—though he couldn't have known it at the time.

Brad's nightly patrol began. He liked the thought of being a guardian angel and took care to keep a prudent distance as he kept watch. Sometimes, he would only need to look after them as they walked across a dark parking lot to their cars. Other times, it was all he could do not to run up behind them and warn them about the danger they were putting themselves in. Even he wouldn't walk the unlit path by Lake Mendota alone.

What were they thinking?

Some nights, if the conditions were right—first floor apartment, no roommate, no dog—he would indulge himself by going into their places. He never went any closer than a bedroom doorway. But, at times, he felt as if he were snuggled next to the Sleeper under her down comforter, her relaxed breath on the back of his neck, a sense of tranquility permeating his body. He didn't even want to touch them, but the calm that enveloped him—a gift, a surprise—was intoxicating.

He told himself that each Sleeper would be his last, but then he would follow one who turned out to sleep so soundly, whose back door practically fell open. He couldn't resist slipping in to watch her for awhile.

Brad made rules for himself: only one a week, always a different neighborhood, never a repeat.

Until this Sleeper, he had kept the pact he'd made with himself, but this was the third time he'd let himself into the tiny house set back from the street. He told himself he kept coming because the lock slipped so easily, because she slept so soundly. But he knew there was something else. He wanted to know why she wore her pale blonde hair cropped shorter than his, why she kept a mother-of-pearl-handled .22 caliber pistol under her nightstand. He wanted to know *her*. Leaving the back door slightly ajar, he glided through the kitchen and stopped for a moment listening for the familiar sound of her breath. When he heard nothing, he stepped closer to the bedroom.

Nothing.

The bottom half of her bed was smooth. He stepped closer.

She wasn't there.

He looked around the room wildly.

He had gotten sloppy. He should have followed her from *Jingles'* as usual. Now he was inside her house, and she could be here, anywhere—asleep on the couch, in the living room *not* asleep. She might open the front door any minute and find him in her hallway wearing night vision goggles and black leather gloves.

As if his imagining had conjured up the real thing, he heard a key in the lock.

He sprinted down the hall and ducked into the bathroom, hid behind the shower curtain. He knew he would be a heart-stopping sight if she pushed it back and found him. He forced himself to breathe more slowly and strained to hear coming-home sounds: door closing, light switch, footsteps, keys on a table. Instead he heard the metronome of a dripping faucet. The house was so quiet he imagined she was sneaking up on *him*, that any minute *she* would throw back the curtain and shout, "Gotcha!" He braced himself for the inevitable discovery… but it never came. The house was as it had been when he'd entered. Empty.

He pushed back the curtain, careful to leave it half-open as he had found it. He knew he should leave, leave and never come back, but he couldn't resist the urge to learn something about the Sleeper before he left. He needed a name for this woman, the one he kept coming back to. He removed his goggles and turned on the light. He opened the medicine cabinet that would tell him about her.

On the top shelf, he found a pill bottle. "Melanie Whittier," he said it aloud, and the medication name: Ambien. That explained the soundness of her sleeping. With Ambien on his side, he could count on many more visits without being discovered. He replaced the bottle, gave one last listen, and headed toward the back door.

As he walked down her street toward home, goggles tucked in his backpack, he tried to figure out why he felt so off-balance, so jittery. Of course, there was the adrenaline from the false alarm, but there was something else. He wasn't edgy like before a mission. Then he realized: he was jealous, like he'd felt when he saw his girlfriend talking to another guy in the high school cafeteria. Tonight, he had come to watch Melanie sleep, and she wasn't there.

Where was she? He pictured her at the bar having a drink with another man, leaning closer to hear him over the music. Brad felt a knot of longing in his stomach and was so preoccupied with the image, that Melanie—the real one—was ten feet away before he realized it. She was walking straight toward him.

Her halo of blonde hair practically glowed. She wore a navy *Jingles'* waitress uniform top. Her tired eyes briefly met his but did not register recognition as he, for no good reason, hoped they would. She didn't look particularly afraid of this stranger in camo walking toward her at bar time. Then he realized why. Her right hand gripped a small can of pepper spray, her index finger poised over the button. The sight made him indescribably sad.

He chanced a smile and a nod. "Hey."

She nodded back but kept walking. Not wanting to scare her, he continued at a steady pace looking straight ahead. Finally, he took off his backpack and sat on a bus stop bench. With patience, he could wait until she was asleep and let himself back into her place. Melanie's place. He could stand silently at the foot of her bed, feeling the peace of her breath washing over him, washing away the guilt that kept him from sleeping and hung on his shoulders like a flak jacket. He pulled his collar to his chin and sat on the bench to wait.

In Brad's dream, a whack on his left foot jacked him up, eyes wide, darting. At the foot of his bed, his squad leader smirked at him.

Brad rolled over, pulled his pillow over his head. "Jesus, Ajax, what the hell?" He felt a smack on his ass.

"Williams, I said we're going on an adventure. That's an order."

Brad knew better than to screw around with Ajax. Rank or not, Ajax was a tough motherfucker who had the power to make his life hell.

"Snag Jimmy and Hawk and meet me outside. Bring your NVG's." Brad dressed quickly, grabbed his goggles, and woke Jimmy and Hawk.

He figured they were headed to a whorehouse, but Brad had no desire to pay for sex, especially with the wrung-out women imported from Turkey for the purpose. He had always found excuses not to go when the rest of the guys went to get laid, but tonight he knew better. The air around Ajax crackled. They headed away from the red-light area down a side street. Ajax stopped at a residence. "We rounded up all the hajis last night but we left the girl here for us." He smiled a sick smile and spit a flake of tobacco off the tip of his tongue.

"Jimmy, take the door." Jimmy leaned back and gave the door a Tai Kwon Do kick. It flew open. The ricochet almost closed it again. Ajax pushed the door open slowly and went ahead. The three stopped and looked at each other. Ajax gave them the "going in" hand signal. Then, as if to remind them he was above protocol, he said aloud, "Come on, you assholes."

Brad hoped to God the girl, whoever she was, would be long gone. Maybe she had fled to her relatives. He made a wish that she had left town altogether. Then he heard a scared squeak and knew Ajax's rabbit waited in the trap.

"I haven't had any pussy in weeks. I get sloppy seconds." Jimmy looked at Brad. "You comin' man?"

"Nah, you go ahead. I'll watch the door." Brad shouldered his weapon and turned his back on what he knew was about to happen. As he leaned on the doorjamb, he glanced to his left and saw a family photograph. The girl would be among the smiling dark-skinned people. He flipped up his goggles and flicked his lighter to see better. Her face came out of the darkness. She was ten or eleven years old, two rope-like braids hanging on either side of her heart-shaped face. I hope she's a lot older than that now, he almost said aloud and then realized the stupidity of the thought. From the photograph, her large brown-black eyes looked straight through him.

Another squeak.

The same squeak of the baby rabbits when Snapper, his childhood beagle, grabbed one up in his jaws and wouldn't let go. But this wasn't a rabbit. Brad closed his eyes and tried to erase the image of Ajax on top of her, bursting her open like a melon. Brad felt the warm stickiness of the rabbit's entrails as he'd tried to stuff them back into the limp body, felt the hot sting of tears as he'd tried to pinch the skin back together.

Squeak.

He flipped his goggles over his eyes, followed the whimpering sound, and assessed the situation. Jimmy and Hawk still wore their goggles but had left their weapons on a table just inside the room. They had their dicks out in anticipation. The girl's wrists were zip-tied above her head. Ajax held handfuls of her hair like horse reins. Ajax's gun lay on the floor beside the mattress. If Brad stepped between Jimmy and Hawk and their weapons, Ajax would be the only one capable of arming himself. His position, however, left him vulnerable. Brad might have a chance to save her.

"Get off her." Brad's voice was barely above a whisper. He set the sight of his weapon just below the strap of Ajax's goggles. Louder this time. "Get. Off. Her." Brad disengaged the gun's safety with a click.

Ajax scanned the floor for his weapon. Jimmy and Hawk looked at Brad then at their weapons. They zipped up and held their palms in the air. Jimmy used his calm-down voice. "Hey, man, take it easy."

Ajax was irate. "What the hell? Put that away right now, soldier, or I'll have your ass in a sling." He didn't bother to stop thrusting while he gave the order.

Slowly, Brad squeezed the trigger, blew Ajax's brains all over the girl, Jimmy and Hawk, too.

Now, he woke with a start, rattling the loose bench of the bus stop. He heard the usual pounding in his ears, but a lightness washed over him. This time, he hadn't been a coward. This time, he hadn't dropped his weapon and run like a scared pussy. This time, he'd had the balls to pull the trigger and wipe the smug grin off Ajax's face. This time, he had set the girl free into the woods to scamper to safety.

Lawn sprinkler. Flashing yellow traffic light. Kid tossing newspapers onto a porch. Pink sky. As Brad scanned his surroundings, he realized where he was. His relief faded.

When he got back to his grandfather's, he opened a Coke, grabbed a handful of Cap'n Crunch and landed in the recliner. The remote was wedged between the cushion and arm.

CNN was in commercial, so he hit the up-channel button. He knew at any moment of any day, he could find war coverage. Lately, he'd had to channel surf a little longer to find something, but not today. A reporter was wrapping up coverage of one of the "deadliest" days of the Iraq war so far. "Thirty-seven American casualties," she said with affected seriousness.

Brad couldn't keep himself from yelling, "Deadliest?! We killed more Iraqis than that before breakfast.

Deadly?! Shit! You don't know deadly!" The last word hung in the room for no one else to hear.

A grim-faced anchor looked out at Brad from the TV screen now. "Since the conflicts began, it has been our custom to present the names and faces of our newly fallen American soldiers. Now then, in silence. . ."

Brad watched as the fresh faces of military personnel flashed on the screen. Each stayed long enough for him to read the name, age and hometown. A feeling of dread settled in his gut. What if one of his buddies looked back at him? Since he'd gotten home, he had been glued to coverage of the war, hoping to get good news or at least do his part to keep track of what was going on. He knew his friends were just an email away, but that would feel too close to being back there.

But now, with enlistment photographs fading in and out in front of him, he was there again, too much of a pussy to stop Ajax from raping the girl.

The faces stopped. The anchor signed off. Credits ran. A voiceover announced underwriters.

Then it occurred to him. In his dread that he would see a buddy's face flash on the screen, he could have missed Ajax's face. Brad had never known Ajax's real name, or if he had, he'd forgotten it. He couldn't recall his hometown or the last name stenciled on the uniform that Brad saw every day. It was one of those things you stop seeing after a while. Ajax was Ajax.

The photographs would have been no help either. The guys he served with looked nothing like their enlistment photos. Men sunburned, with sand in the creases of their skin, looked nothing like the fresh-shaved kids in the photos against blue backgrounds and with a flag behind their left shoulders. His fellow soldiers looked so different, in fact, that once in a while, someone's enlistment picture would end up on a bulletin board in the mess tent with the words, "Guess who?" under it. Nine times out of ten, the twenty-five dollar bet went unclaimed.

The more he thought about the possibility of Ajax being among the deceased, the more excited Brad became. His lightness returned with the thought of Ajax's balls blown off by an IED, Ajax prevented forever from hurting another little girl. Brad stood up and walked toward the TV as if to tell it the news. "Ajax could be dead." And then, because the sound of it was so beautiful, so poetic, he changed the words. "Ajax is dead! Dead! Dead! Dead!"

The more he recited the mantra, the truer it became. "Ajax is dead."

He paced the room with thundering steps and cranked his hand in the air like he had made a three-pointer. But there was no crowd to cheer him, no teammates to celebrate with him. He ran out to the front yard and let out a grand hoot. No neighbors came to their windows to frown or smile in amusement at the camo-clad man with a grown-out brush cut and dark circles under his eyes as he did a victory dance around the yard.

He bounded back into the house and, for a moment, considered the fact that he could easily confirm Ajax's death by turning on the computer and doing a quick search. But he knew he didn't need to. Ajax was dead.

He had to be.

Brad took a hot shower and fell naked into bed. He slept the sleep of the dead and woke to a dark house. The digital clock read 10:18 p.m.

A lone car sat in the lot next to the bar. Without his goggles, he couldn't see the make or model, but it looked like the same one he had seen there other nights. The waistband on his jeans was snugger than when he had first gotten back. His button-down felt like a kiss. He imagined himself walking into *Jingles'* and grabbing a seat at the bar. He would sit at the end where the waitress—Melanie—would be picking up drinks for the customers at her tables, if any besides Brad came in. From the looks of it, it would be a pretty quiet night.

Or maybe she would be in the kitchen rolling utensils inside napkins, flirting with the cook. Brad's body tensed, and he tried to push away the thought. As he started to second-guess his decision, he realized he was holding his breath, a sure sign he was losing control of the situation. He had done this in Basic and later during particularly dangerous missions.

He exhaled and stood up. Took measured breaths. Retucked his shirt. His feet felt like foreigners in his old Nikes after months in combat boots. He walked down the slope, eyes fixed on the door of the bar. If he could keep his objective in mind, fear wouldn't get the best of him.

"Hey." The bartender tossed a cardboard coaster on the bar. "How ya doin'?"

"Good."

"What can I get ya?"

Brad squinted at the tapper handles. "I'll have a Leinie's. Your grill still open?"

The bartender grabbed a glass and gave the tapper a pull. He looked at the clock.

"You still got fifteen minutes. I'll have Mel get you a menu."

Brad sat on a barstool for stability. In his imagined version of the scene, this was how it went—only he never actually thought it *would* go this way. He took a pull on the cold beer, his first since he had been stateside. It tasted like spring.

A menu appeared from behind him. "Here you go." Her voice took him by surprise. It was solid, deeper than he had expected. It was a voice you could tie your boat to. Brad resisted the urge to turn and look her full in the face. Better to take it slow. "Thanks."

"I'll be back to take your order."

Our Hoyles

Nine hearts. Dang. My husband's always doing that, overbidding me when he knows full well I can make my bid and he's got diddly-squat. Of course, nine hearts is the perfect bid—for Ed. If he wins the round, he's a hero for pulling it off with a hand like a foot. That's what we call it when our cards stink. If we get bumped, he can blame it on me, say that I inkled wrong, that I made him think I could get more tricks than I really could. Never mind that I bid *spades*. That fact won't make a bit of difference to him when we replay the hand at the top of our lungs after Dan and Jean have gone home. Either way, nine hearts makes him look good and me look bad.

"You must have a mittful of hearts." Dan slides the blind over to Ed.

If you ask me, taking away a perfectly good seven spades bid from me, his partner, is definitely not on the up-and-up as far as Hoyle is concerned. Sure, none of us have read the book that spells out the rules of card games, but we Simpsons have our own unwritten guide. We call them Our Hoyles: never send a boy to do a man's work; never overbid your partner in a different suit unless you're positive you can win the hand all by yourself; and never, *never* overplay your partner's card if he has already won the trick.

Ed likes to break at least one of Our Hoyles every time we play cards, usually the second one. Like he's doing now.

He whistles through his teeth while he pulls the blind toward himself. Before he starts picking up the cards, he slides his empty tumbler across the table at me, "While you're up." He doesn't look up from his hand.

Out the corner of my eye, I can see Jean's jaw tighten. She puts down her cards and takes a deep breath. I know there's no love lost between her and Ed. The only reason she still comes to play cards every other Saturday night is for me, to keep me sane. But, more and more, I see her losing patience with Ed and his cocky attitude.

Years ago, I stopped confiding in Jean about Ed. It just got her all riled up about how he was treating her baby sister, and it got me feeling all guilty because I wasn't strong enough to stand up to him or to leave him. But yesterday, I snapped and had to talk to someone.

Ed and I had just gotten done arguing about whether or not we could afford braces for Stephanie when Jean called. As I picked up the phone, I noticed a new gun case propped up in the corner of the living room. "I can't believe it. He bought himself a new deer rifle." I didn't even realize I'd said it out loud until I heard Jean's voice on the other end.

"I don't know why you stay with that man, Delores."

I ask Dan to scooch in so I can get around the table to get Ed's brandy and water. He likes them dark— just a splash of water and a few ice cubes—the color of weak iced tea, a little darker than apple juice. As I rinse out his glass, my mind jumps to the liquid drain opener under the sink. I've been having terrible, terrible thoughts like this one lately. I know it's awful, but I start to wonder how much it would take to poison him. Would the strength of the brandy cover up the taste of a teaspoon or two of the Drano? I am so preoccupied with the wondering that I realize I have brought Ed's glass with me into the bathroom when I go to take a tinkle. There are lots of other lethal cocktails in here: toilet bowl cleaner, bleach, even my anti-anxiety pills in the right amount could kill him.

"Hey, what's taking so long? I'm ready to win this hand in here!"

I flush the toilet, splash water on my face and return to the kitchen to finish making Ed's drink.

"Sorry," I call from the kitchen. "Does anyone else need anything while I'm up?"

"You don't need to wait on *me*, Delores." Jean's comment is aimed at Ed, but its meaning isn't lost on me. I pour Fritos into a bowl and return to the game.

As Dan stands up so I can get back to my chair, Ed is already slamming down his lead card. It's gonna be one of those hands where he slams down lead after lead not bothering to pick up the tricks he's already won. Now, some people hate the lay-down hand, and I can't disagree. It's completely unsatisfying to watch someone lay down their perfectly fanned cards, with no doubt that they would have taken all the tricks if the hand had been played out one at a time, but I have to say I hate the slam-playing even more. I know Ed does this to try to psych out the other team, make them feel like he's so confident about winning it doesn't matter what they throw on his leads, he's gonna take the tricks anyway. The funny thing is we've all been playing with him long enough to know what the slam-lead means: he doesn't have the cards to win. He's hoping someone will slough off the wrong card and make a dinky one of his good.

Jean is rolling her eyes, taking her sweet time throwing each card on Ed's leads. So far, it doesn't look like she has anything to stop him, although she is staying with him trump-for-trump. Dan, on the other hand, ran out of trump after the first trick. It looks like if anyone is going to stop Ed, it will have to be Jean.

Or me.

I've been counting trump—something Ed refuses to do, saying that's the way dim bulbs play—and with the slap of his card on the table, I realize what has just happened. He's played himself out of trump and his highest card, which is on the table now, is the king of spades. He's counting on me to hold back the ace and let him take the trick. Jean plays her nine of spades. I know Dan is powerless. He throws a red four. According to our third Hoyle, I should let Ed take it. That would sew up the hand for us.

I glance at the rifle in the corner, its *Bill's House of Guns* tag mocking me. I buck the third Hoyle and throw my ace. He looks at me in disbelief. I shrug. "I had to follow suit, sorry."

I lead a small club knowing that Jean will take the trick with her remaining trump and we'll be bumped. Ed doesn't know what hit him until I throw my six of spades—the card I should have thrown on his king. He glares across the table; a vein pops in his neck.

I want to tell him he's not the only one who can buck Our Hoyles, but I watch silently as he lifts his drink to his lips. He bares his teeth slightly as he pours the liquid into his mouth like he's trying to drink the whole thing in one gulp. He sucks air through his teeth as he slams the empty glass on the table.

"That drink tasted like piss."

Justice

I've never been a God-fearing man. God-avoiding is more like it, at least since my mama died all those years ago. The day she was laid to rest, the Lord and I parted ways. But on the Sunday of the Packers-Vikings game, all that changed.

I was heading home from *Smitty's*. The guys on AM620 were going on about what a picture-perfect game the Packers had played.

"It's a goddamn miracle is what it is!" I said even though there was no one in the pickup with me. I was feeling that good. I guess the round of shots on the house for every Packer touchdown made me a little more talkative than usual.

Then, it happened. The Lord Jesus reached down His finger and pushed my gas gauge needle over to E. It was like I watched it move.

Now, usually I just keep driving when I get close to E, but He pushed it so far, my fuel light went on. I knew I couldn't make it across town to *Heathen Hank's* (that's what we call Hank's place as a joke), so I had to pull into *Andersen's New Life Christian Kwik Stop*. As a rule,

I tried to stay away from the place, but I was practically driving on fumes. I put in 10 bucks' worth and headed inside to pay. Not that I cared, but I stopped to tuck in my shirt before I went inside, like I was going into a church or something.

The store wasn't anything like I'd pictured it. No workers wearing white robes and sandals, no shellacked praying hands. It looked like any other convenience store, except the workers wore matching blue golf shirts with a white fish over the pocket. Not counting the Bible verse ashtrays, the place didn't seem to have any religious knickknacks. What I did find surprised me, and that is how the Lord won me over after all those years of giving each other the silent treatment.

First, I checked the coolers. Not only did the Lord believe in beer, He stocked twice as much high-alcohol Ice beer as the regular stuff. Since He'd brought me there and cases were on discount, I took that as a sign.

Speaking of signs, "Cigarettes: Lowest Legal Prices" caught my eye. *Good thing the Lord respects the law.* I could almost hear Him whisper, "I'd give 'em to ya for free if I could, but the law's the law. You understand." Who could argue with that? I asked for two cartons.

What I saw next completely won me over: just on the other side of the lotto machine, I saw the corner of a magazine. I started to ask if they had any of them titty magazines and caught myself. I was in a Christian store, after all. I smoothed down my hair. "You don't happen to have any *adult* magazines back there, do ya?"

"Why, yes, sir." The clerk looked at me a little funny, then smiled. "But we do keep them behind the counter where the kids can't see them. Which one would you like?"

Now I couldn't ask that bright-faced kid for *Pussies Galore*, so I just said, "*Playboy.*" There it was. The trifecta.

I paid for my beer, smokes, porno and gas and winked at the clerk. "God Bless!"

Next morning, I woke up in the recliner. My foot kicked an empty Icehouse when I stood up, and I had to think for a minute where it came from. I usually drink Red, White & Blue. Then I saw a cig burned to the nub right next to yesterday's sports section on the end table. *Shit, one more inch and the house woulda gone up like a tinderbox.* I fell asleep with a burning Marlboro in my hand and lived to tell about it. Maybe now that me and the Lord was on a first-name basis, He decided to watch out for me. I figured He must've had something really important for me to do if He was going to all this trouble. I felt a rush of adrenaline wondering what my mission would be.

After I pissed and swished out my mouth, I put on a clean t-shirt, lit up a smoke, and decided to read the paper, not just the sports section either. I would start on page one and wait for the Lord to give me another sign.

I woke up again with the right side of my face resting on page three. On page two, under a story about some church scandal, my eyes caught a picture of one of them crazy towel heads. He pointed his finger up in the air. I swear, I could hear him shout. "Death to America." I blinked a couple times trying to figure out what this meant. Maybe I was supposed to join the PLO, whatever the hell that was. Or maybe I was supposed to join the army and kill some Iraqis. But, no, if that was it, the President himself woulda been talking to me from the newspaper.

I sat up and checked the time. "Dammit!"

"What's the excuse this time?" The owner's nephew, Barry, looked down his nose at me.

When he'd first started as supervisor, he cut me some slack about being late. First, he gave me "options." Maybe I wanted to start my shift later, he'd said. I tried, but I was late anyway. That's just the kind of guy I am.

Next he sicked Betty the Drug Counselor from HR on me. I'm not stupid. I knew how to answer her questions where she was trying to get me to admit alcohol was ruining my life. After a while, she gave up and handed me her card. "If you ever decide to get help, Russ, give me a call."

She must've told Barry I was a lost cause. After that, he just kept track of my reasons—"excuses," he called them—for being late. I knew it wouldn't be long before I got put on probation.

This was starting to bug me, but then I remembered about the Lord's plan. *Hey, maybe the Lord* wants *me to lose this job so I can do His work. Whatever that is.* Or maybe I was supposed to save Barry's soul by introducing him to the Big Guy. Barry's "what-now-fuck-up?" face interrupted my thoughts. No, the Lord couldn't possibly want a twit like Barry on his team.

"Fell asleep reading the paper," is what I told him before I punched in and headed to my spot on the line. I didn't have to look at him to know he was shaking his head and writing in my file. The tightass.

One morning a couple weeks later, still drunk from the night before, I heard a knock on the front door. By the time I got there, two guys were already picking their way back down the porch stairs. When I opened the screen door, they spun around and put on holy faces.

"Sir." The little one made it to me first. "I'm Matthias and this is Jebediah. How are you today?" He didn't wait for an answer. "Do you have a personal relationship with the Lord Jesus Christ?"

Matthias' introduction gave Jebediah a chance to get to the top of the stairs holding out a pamphlet. I didn't answer right away. I was mesmerized by the whiteness of their shirts, those crisp black ties. I tried to focus on the black of their pants, but it felt like one of them black holes you get sucked into and can't get out. I steadied myself on the doorjamb. They both looked a little scared. Jebediah stuck the pamphlet back into his bag and turned to leave. Matthias wasn't far behind.

"Yes, gentlemen, I do." They stopped. "The Lord has been giving me signs for the past two weeks. If you'll come in and drink a beer with me, I'd like to tell you all about it." I muffled a burp.

Matthias and Jebediah made a huddle. It looked like they didn't know what to do with my invitation. I couldn't hear Jebediah, but I did hear Matthias using words like "soul" and "mission" and "salvation." Or maybe that was Jebediah. Them black and white outfits got confusing after awhile.

"I'll let you guys figure it out. I gotta take a piss." I left them on the edge of the top step. When I came out a few minutes later, they were gone.

When I finally got to work, Barry added "Talking to Jehovah's Witnesses" to my list of excuses for being late. Next thing I know, I'm out of a job.

"Russ, you asshole." Hank's voice interrupted my slow drink of coffee.

"Where the hell you been? I ain't seen you at the station for a couple a weeks at least."

Ever since the *Kwik Stop*, I'd been avoiding Hank. I figured I'd be safe at *The Greasy Spoon* at 11:00 on a Thursday. "Me? What are you doing here in the middle of the morning? Who's watching the shop?"

Sandy filled a cup and slid it toward Hank. "Donovan's shittin' kid. I hired him to help out mornings since the bastard got kicked out of school." Hank dribbled coffee down his chin. "Dammit. Got my damn tooth drilled this morning."

I never had one conversation with Hank where he didn't curse at least once a sentence. It got to be contagious, and, even though I'd been trying to take it easy on my language since I joined the Lord's team and all, I just couldn't help myself. "Shit. Nothing worse than getting your tooth drilled." My head throbbed with the thought of it, but I wanted to stay on the subject of his teeth. I didn't want to have to explain why I hadn't been filling my tank at his station.

"Yeah, what about you? Shouldn't you be at the mill?"

"Ahk. Barry gave me my walkin' papers." I took another drink hoping the caffeine would kick in and clear my head.

"Hell. I s'pose you don't go through much gas when you ain't got a job to go to." He tried to take another drink of coffee. "Jesus H. Christ!" He grabbed for a napkin to wipe off his workshirt. The TV behind the counter caught his attention. "Look at that, will ya?" The sound was turned down, but Hank seemed to know what the news story was about. He let out a disgusted grunt. "Who'd believe a thing like that? A priest and little boys. You've gotta be goddamn kidding me."

My cheeks got hot all of a sudden. I grunted, too. I didn't know the details of the scandal but something made me want to end the conversation. Fast. My heart was pounding in my ears.

"Well." I pushed my cup across the counter. "Thanks, Sandy."

My hands shook as I pulled out my wallet. Hank put his hand on my shoulder. "I got it." He slid my bill under his coffee cup. "You need anything, Russ, you just ask. I give Donovan's fuck-up kid a job, I sure as hell can find something for you."

I felt about as low as dirt. Here was Hank offering to help me through a rough patch when I'd been buying my gas, smokes, beer and even bread from Les. Jr. Hell, I was on a first name basis with Zach and Bryan, the kids who worked at the *Kwik Stop*.

"Thanks. I do appreciate that. Got a few things in the hopper. Should be okay."

I was glad I didn't have to make up an excuse for Barry that day. I just felt too damn bad. Maybe the Lord's full-court press was all in my head. Maybe He was just messing with me.

I sat in my truck, smoking for a long time before I started her up. When I was done driving, I found myself at the cemetery. It took some doing to find Daddy's grave probably because when we buried him, we were hunched up under a tarp that blocked the view of the rest of the cemetery. I found him, though, and stood where I figured his feet were underneath the ground. I looked in the direction of Mama's grave best I could remember, hoping that Daddy could see Mama's resting place from here—even though he wasn't baptized and couldn't be buried in the Catholic section next to her. When I looked to the left, my eyes got stuck on a bright red maple.

It was bigger now, but I knew it was the tree I'd stared at through the service at Mama's grave, squeezing my jaws together to try to keep from crying. And throwing up.

"Son, say Thank you to Father Townsend." Daddy's hand felt like a rock on my shoulder. I opened my mouth but the priest's red ears stopped me. I looked at my shoes.

"That's all right, Del. He's grieving is all." Father Townsend put his hand on my other shoulder and then I did puke. Right on the priest's shoes. I should have gotten a kick out of remembering the look on his face, but instead, my jaws felt like a vice. *Why in the hell would Daddy want me to thank that bastard?*

"Which bastard would that be?" The gravelly voice made me jump. I didn't realize I'd talked out loud. I turned around to see Happy Mulligan leaning on a shovel. "If it ain't Del Schneider's boy. You look just like the old man."

He probably meant it as a compliment, but it sure didn't feel like it.

"Hey, Hap," I gave him a nod.

Happy buried everyone who died for miles around. When he buried Mama, he was just plain old. He was ancient when he buried Daddy and so old now he looked like a ghost. The handle of his shovel looked bigger around than his forearms.

"Well? Which bastard you talking about?"

My face got hot. "Never mind." Happy tilted his head and looked at me sideways. Hoping to distract him, I reached for a cigarette, shook one halfway out of the pack and held it forward. He refused with a quick shake of his head. As I lit mine, I changed my mind. "Okay," I said, "Father Townsend, that son of a bitch. Why would Daddy want me to thank *him*?"

"Come have a drink with me and the Mrs." Happy headed toward the Catholic section of the cemetery. I'd never heard of a Mrs. Mulligan, so I was confused until Happy stopped next to a headstone that said "Martha Mulligan, 1919-1945." He opened a flask. "To those who've gone before us." He lifted it first to his wife's stone, then to the smaller one next to it. He nodded in the general direction of Mama's, then Daddy's, graves. Took a big swig and handed it to me.

My hands shook as I reached for it. The heat of the liquor on the back of my throat almost made me gag, but by the time it hit my stomach, I felt my whole body relax. Happy reached for the flask, capped it, and put it back in his pocket.

"One a day, that's what me and the Mrs. agreed on. I've kept my promise since the day we said, 'I do.'"

"A promise like that would have saved my daddy's life."

"The way your hands is shakin' it seems the same might be said for you. What are you now? Same age as when your daddy died?"

I didn't want to admit I was more than a few years younger, but I didn't have the energy to make up a lie. "Not by a long shot." I nodded toward Happy's pocket. "You know, *I* didn't make any promises to Mrs. Mulligan. You think I could see that flask again?"

Happy hesitated then reached into his pocket. "Not enough to get lit up on anyway." He took out a hand trimmer and started snipping the already short grass around Mrs. Mulligan's stone. "Besides, I'm keeping my promise to the Mrs. so I can see her in heaven when I kick the bucket myself. Burying her and the baby in holy ground is the most important gift I ever gave her. She'd tell ya that if you could ask her."

Trying to figure out what this had to do with thanking Father Townsend, I capped the empty flask and handed it back to him.

"It's the last gift your daddy could give to your mama, and he needed Father Townsend in order to give it to her. That's why he wanted you to say thank you." He wiped the blades of the hand trimmer on his pants, closed the safety lock and hung it back on his belt loop. "Might not seem important to you, but, believe me, it meant the world to your mama." He started to walk away. "You take care now, Rusty."

"Hap?"

He turned around. "Yeah?"

"What ever happened to the priest?"

He rubbed his chin. "Transferred to another parish—"

He looked like he had more to say, then changed his mind.

"I'll see you 'round, Rusty."

He was gone before I could ask him anything else. By the time he disappeared over the hill, I wasn't even sure he'd been there at all. It was less than a hundred yards to Mama's grave.

May Catherine Schneider
1940–1972
Loved in life, she has found eternal happiness

"How could she be any happier in the hard ground than she was fussin' over her geraniums?" I'd asked my daddy while we were trying to figure out what to say on her headstone. Daddy, who was never at a loss for words, got real quiet. I'd never seen him cry before, so I wasn't sure if his pinched-up face could even qualify as crying. It was like he was a shaken up can of beer trying not to explode.

He pretty much stayed drunk from that day on. It wasn't long before we figured out that a beer before bed helped me sleep right through the nightmares and even put an end to the bedwetting that started up after the funeral.

On my 18th birthday, we cracked open a case together when I got home from the mill. We were practically three-sheets by the time we heard the screen door open and close real quick. I looked out the window and saw Edna Marshall from across the street walking away from the porch. A postcard sat on the throw rug in the entryway.

"Mrs. Marshall hopes to see us this year for Easter mass."

I handed Daddy the card. He pulled out two more beers from the cooler.

"The ol' biddy. She's probably been keeping attendance records on us all these years since your mama died." He lit the card on fire and let it burn until it was small enough to put in the glass ashtray. We watched it until the *bweep* of the smoke detector got to be too much.

"I got it." I stood on a chair and pulled the battery out, leaving it open so we'd remember to put it back together when the smoke cleared.

When I sat down again, Daddy poured us both another shot of Beam, and we drank them watching the smoke drift up in spirals. I was trying *not* to remember the last time we were in Holy Redeemer Church. I figured Daddy was thinking on it, too, but when he talked again, it was a sweet memory of Mama, how she smiled on the day I was born. "A smile like that, Rusty, I never did see. She had the face of Mary herself." I ached for him to give me some more good memories of Mama, but all I got was silence the length of a whole can of beer and then some.

"I don't care what that priest said. She'da gone to heaven no matter what." Daddy picked up the Beam bottle and took a long pull on it. Not just a tug but a series of gulps, 1, 2, 3.

By then the sun was completely gone. Neither of us got up to turn on a light. We just sat in the dark with the cooler between us. The beers shifted as the ice melted. I didn't know how to ask him. "Whaddya mean, 'No matter what?'"

By the time I figured out what to say, his answer was a snore. I pulled an afghan up to his chin and went to bed.

When I dragged myself into the living room next morning, I could tell he hadn't moved an inch all night. The blanket hung under his chin just like I left it. As I got closer, the smell hit me. He'd shit himself. The stench made me gag. "Oh, geez, Daddy. C'mon, get up." Then it hit me how quiet the room was. No snoring, just the clock on the mantle.

I gagged again and threw up into the closest thing I could find, the cooler. I knew he was dead, knew it in my bones. *Daddy's gonna kill me for this alcohol abuse.* I emptied my guts on the three cans of Red, White & Blue floating inside.

When they shut the lid on his coffin, he looked as withered as one of them dried up apple-face people they raffle off at church festivals. There wasn't much for Daddy to leave me—just the house and an old piece-of-shit pickup—that and a sour taste in my mouth. The whole time Harvey Bartlett from the funeral home was babbling about ashes and dust at Daddy's graveside, I was glad Mama wasn't there to see it. Glad she couldn't see the mess I was after three days of drinking toasts to Daddy.

I turned to look in the direction of Daddy's grave and I realized this was exactly where I'd stood through the graveside service for Mama. I knew if I looked up from the ground, I would see those red maple leaves, the same color as Father Townsend's ears. I tried to keep my eyes on the grass, but something pulled them toward the tree. My heartbeat picked up.

Even with my eyes shut tight, there they were. Like I couldn't stop gawking at an accident or watching a movie even though I knew the ending would give me nightmares. My mind was back at the rectory where I first noticed them damned ears.

Mama cleaned the rectory once a week as part of her service to the church. Until she got the job, the other ladies of the parish took turns. But once Father Townsend tasted Mama's meatloaf, he told her that, with cooking that divine, it must be her heavenly calling to be his weekly housekeeper and cook.

"My meatloaf!" She shook her head when she told us about it. "Who would imagine meatloaf would be my gift to God?"

On Saturdays, Mama hummed hymns and wore a fresh apron. She made up two meatloaves, one for us and one for the priest. I'd help her pack her tote bag with the meatloaf, two baking potatoes and a can of beans, and then we'd walk to the park down the street from the rectory.

Duke and Arney knew to meet me for a game of Pickle, and Mama didn't have to worry about me getting into trouble while she did her work.

I wanted to stop the movie there. Keep hold of the way she rubbed the top of my head before she kissed my cheek. Keep that fresh Mama smell in my nose. That's where it always stopped for me. Then the theater got black and we were standing at Mama's grave.

Something about being in the cemetery that day kept the reel going, and I knew I didn't have a choice in the matter. I had to watch it until the end. And the projector played it in slow motion.

That day, Duke and Arney got called in early for supper, and I headed to the rectory to use the bathroom. Bouncing from one foot to the other, I knocked on the screen door. I heard the vacuum down the hall, so I stepped into the entryway. "Mama?" The smell of onions and ground beef made my mouth water.

All I could hear was the vacuum. When I rounded the corner into the study, first thing I saw was the nozzle on the fancy rug. I heard a grunt and saw Father Townsend's ears blazing as he pushed himself at my mama. Her back was jammed up against the wall of books. At first, I didn't realize what I was seeing. Mama's eyes squeezed shut. She was biting her lower lip. Her forehead looked like one big worried knot. I dropped my eyes and noticed the priest's pants at his ankles, his flabby white butt cheeks squeezing together as he pushed and pushed and pushed. I thought he'd lift her right off the ground. I took a step forward and stopped. I didn't know what to do to save her. I didn't try.

Piss ran down my leg.

I bumped into the wall and ran back to the empty playground. Crying like a baby, I hung from the monkey bars trying to dry out my jeans before Mama came out. When she did, I realized my pants could have been on fire and she wouldn't have noticed. Her eyes were red and panicky. She smoothed her hair over and over, tucked it behind her ears, retucked it, took a comb out of her purse, and combed it until I thought it would fall out right there on the playground. Without a word, we headed home.

As I walked up the front steps behind her, I got a whiff of old books, burnt candles, and communion wine. The Mama smell had evaporated.

When I got back to the truck, I had to turn on my wipers to clear the dew before I pulled into the road again. I turned them on high to block out the sound of the priest's voice, "Of course, if she *had* taken her own life, she couldn't be buried in sacred ground, but there is no proof May didn't just get confused about her sleeping pills and accidentally..." I closed my eyes to block out the sight of him holding up his hand. "No need to thank me, Del." I rolled down the windows and hit the gas.

At the *Kwik Stop*, I opened my wallet to pay for a tall boy. All I found was an old receipt, the bent business card of Betty the Drug Counselor, and the prayer card from Mama's funeral. Zach voided out the sale while I went to my truck to scrounge around in the glove compartment for some change. I came up short, so I started up the truck and headed for *Smitty's*, the only joint in town where I could still run a tab. And drink in peace.

Next thing I knew, a vice was squeezing my brains out through my eyes.

Thump. Thump. Thump.

I had fallen asleep on the floor by the couch. The fingers on my left hand tingled, and I had to piss something fierce.

"Mr. Schneider? Russ?" a muffled voice called from outside. "Are you all right? It's me, Betty Teasdale."

Thump. Thump. Thump.

I had no idea who Betty Teasdale was but pulled myself to my knees, then my feet. I opened the door and headed for the bathroom.

When I came back, she held out a Styrofoam cup and a white bag. "I thought you might need this." My mouth was too dried out to water, but the donuts smelled good. As I took the lid off to drink, my hand shook and spilled hot coffee all over my pants.

"Good God dammit!"

"Oh, dear." Betty disappeared down the hall and came back with a dishtowel. "The only AA meeting this morning is over in Waupun. We need to leave in five minutes. I'll be in the car."

She didn't wait around for me to ask what the hell she was talking about, so I inhaled the Boston cream wearing one boot, wondering where the other one went. After I brushed my teeth, I combed water through my hair and found the other boot. I was tempted to crawl under the covers and call it a day, but a car horn beeped and Betty flashed her lights. I fell straight asleep in the passenger's seat before we hit County M.

I smelled Mama before I saw her, smelled the special perfume she wore to church on Sundays. She sat at her vanity looking in a mirror. The face that stared back looked like all its muscles decided to take the day off, but her eyes darted all over, at her hairline, then her chin, then her cheeks, then one eye, then the other. They were out of control, especially compared to how still the rest of her face was.

She grabbed a rosary hanging on the edge of the mirror and held it with both hands. For a minute, it looked like she was going to start in on an *Our Father*, but instead her shoulder blades squeezed together as she pulled the rosary apart, first the round part, then the straight strand. Finally, she ripped the dangling cross from its chain. She used it to scratch deep cuts in each of her wrists. Then I noticed the steaming meatloaf next to her hairbrush. The smell of blood and onions was so real I knew this couldn't be a dream.

She picked up the pan and walked over to a figure on the bed, a lump under the covers. I thought it was Daddy, but when he rolled over, the ears gave him away. Seeing Mama, his eyes got huge, and he opened his mouth to scream but no sound came out. She pinched off a handful of meatloaf, crammed it down his throat, and stuffed another clump straight into his ears, first one, then the other. Next, she started in on his nostrils. Even though his body squirmed, he didn't try to get away. I was so surprised I hardly noticed her gentle voice saying the words of the *Hail Mary*. No emotion, just like she said it in church every Sunday of her whole life.

"Now and at the hour of our death." She finished with the meatloaf exactly at the "Amen."

She wiped both her bloody wrists across his forehead and clapped her hands together like she was brushing off flour, smoothed her apron and looked me straight in the eye. She tipped her head toward her victim, "You know what to do," she said without moving her lips.

"But they'll never believe a drunk like me." My voice was a whisper.

"You'll make them believe you." Her calm face felt like a wave through my body.

A car door slammed. I wiped drool from the corner of my mouth and followed Betty through the door at the side of the church.

I knew what I needed to do.

Right Place, Right Time

CJ has never been so aware of her body. The deep breaths that cause her chest to rise and fall, the slight tremble of her hands, the slickness of the unfamiliar lipstick, the pulse and slight moistness between her legs. If she has ever felt this hyperaware and nervous before, she can't remember it. Maybe when she was with Arturo, but that was over twenty years ago.

Pretending to window-shop in front of a shoe store, she occasionally looks across the street at the café where she agreed to meet Ray, one of those new places with couches and jazz music that the young teachers at school talk about. No one has gone in for the past ten minutes. *Maybe he's already in there waiting for me. Maybe my watch is off and he is already taking the last swallow of coffee, wiping his mouth, and standing up to leave.* She turns from the shoe store and dashes across the street, nearly getting hit by a rusty Cutlass. Impossibly, her heart beats faster.

When she safely arrives at the curb, she slows down again. If he steps out of the café now, she'll be close enough to stop him. *Ray?* she'll say, *I'm so sorry. I hope you didn't think I'd stood you up.* But no one comes.

The bell over the door rings as she pulls it open, the bitter smell of coffee hitting her nose as she scans the shop. The only other patron is a woman who looks up from her laptop when she sees CJ enter.

"Hi, welcome to *Jitterz*, can I start a drink for you?"

"Uhm, yeah." CJ looks up at the menu on the wall. She really doesn't know how to order in a place like this. Back home, the most creative the coffee gets is the café au lait at the McDonald's out on Highway 14 or the hazelnut Cremora in the teachers' lounge at school. "I'm supposed to meet someone here. A man?" She realizes she doesn't even know what he looks like. On the online poetry class bulletin board where they met, he hadn't bothered to upload a photo to replace the yellow smiley face default icon. Neither had she, for that matter. Nine weeks later, the other class members joked that she and Ray must be twins because they both looked like they should be slashing prices in a WalMart commercial. Now she can't even give a hair color or height—or even race for that matter—to the girl behind the counter to identify Ray.

The counter girl fiddles with her eyebrow ring. "I just got on but I haven't waited on any guys since I got here." She pauses. "Weird." Another pause. "Do you need a minute?"

"Huh?" CJ doesn't know what to make of the question. She is still deciding whether to be disappointed he hasn't come or hopeful that he still might.

"Do you know what you want?"

Silence.

"A coffee drink?" Her eyebrows are up, her look impatient.

CJ looks at the chalkboard behind the girl and tries to discern between a latte and a café au lait. "Maybe I'll just get a regular coffee."

With one eye on the door, CJ fiddles with the thermos carafe marked "½ and ½" and lets the small dribble that remains into her cup. She chooses one of the smaller tables on the wall and slides onto the bench down the way from the woman who is still tapping on her laptop.

CJ takes a big gulp of coffee and immediately regrets it. Stupid. Usually she puts so much cream in her coffee that it's practically cool enough to chug from the first drink. But now her eyes water, and she struggles with the decision to hold the scalding liquid in her mouth or just to swallow it and hope for the best. She swallows, but the damage has been done. She tries to suck air over her tongue to cool it. When she closes her mouth again, she can feel the injured taste buds scraping the roof of her mouth. She needs some water, but the counter girl has disappeared. There doesn't seem to be a place where she can help herself.

Stop. Breathe.

She reaches into her bag and pulls out the copy of the last email Ray sent before they set out to meet. She printed it, highlighted "*Jitterz*" and the address, and stapled it to both the MapQuest and Google Maps directions. No doubt about it, she is in the right place. She looks at the date on the email, looks again at the time. She is in the right place and at the right time. If he walks in right now, he'll be twenty minutes late. This could be explained in any number of ways: traffic, a flat tire. She gave him her cell phone number almost as an afterthought before she had powered down the computer in the English office at school. Now she can't imagine why he hasn't phoned.

Hoping that she has absentmindedly left her cell on vibrate and missed his call, she reaches into her bag again. The pocket where she usually keeps the phone is empty. The main compartment where she sometimes tosses it when she's in a hurry is clear, too. Then she remembers it sitting next to her keyboard back at the office.

She had only meant to charge it for a few minutes before she left. Her nerves must have gotten the best of her.

"Damn."

The woman a few tables over looks CJ's way. CJ flushes. She didn't mean to swear out loud.

Laughter enters even before the door opens. Four kids, just a year or two older than CJ's students, tumble into the café. They wear all manner of clothes: an argyle sweater vest with ripped jeans, rainbow toe socks with flip flops, a crocheted hat, a too- big oxford with the Ralph Lauren logo modified to look like the polo player is holding a placard with a peace sign on it. They choose a table across from CJ.

As she watches them, she notices how much looser their boundaries are even than the juniors and seniors in her classroom. The girl with curly red hair has thrown her leg across the lap of the boy on her right while the Asian girl on her left twists her friend's orange ringlet around her finger. There is a comfort between them all that reflects either an easy platonic relationship or a sexual one. She can't tell which. Though she works with young people every day, CJ simply can't imagine how they have come to feel so comfortable with their sexuality. Much, much more comfortable than she ever did. Even Angela, the new teacher in the department, thinks nothing of sharing the most intimate details of her sex life with Todd. Every time he drops in, CJ flushes with the knowledge that he gets horny during thunderstorms and uses Blue Rocket condoms.

"Were you ever married?" Angela once posed the question as a child asks a grandparent about how things were in the olden days. CJ could tell she was looking for a distraction from the essays she was grading. Mid-pile was the only time Angela struck up a conversation with CJ, and then it was never apropos of anything.

Had she ever been married? She didn't want to tell Angela about Arturo, the engagement, her cold feet at the thought of spending the rest of her life in Brazil after having lived there for six months on a trial basis. Did she really want to share the story of how, after months of soul searching, she had ultimately decided that she *would* escape her parents' house, marry Arturo, and live the life of a well-off housewife in a suburb of São Paulo, only to have her letter cross with Arturo's own. His was accompanied by a photograph of him and another handsome man in front of the *Museu de Arte de São Paulo* where Arturo worked.

My Dear Constance, (Arturo never called her CJ like everyone else did.)
I hope this letter finds you well and that you are having a

good life. As you know, I felt very sad when you decided that you could not live in São Paulo and be my wife. My parents, too, had hoped you would be happy here and give them many grandchildren. Alas, it seems we have both disappointed them, for I have found someone new, my soulmate as they say. Gilberto and I have found great happiness together despite my parents' disapproval.

I know you will find this news shocking, Constance. I was surprised myself to feel attraction for another man, but when it felt so right, I just knew it.

I tell you this not to make you feel badly, dear Constance, but to tell you that you made the right decision in not marrying me. What if I had met Gilberto after you had moved here? What if we'd had children together? That would have hurt you even more than this letter might right now.

May you find the kind of love and oneness with someone that I have found with Gilberto. You deserve it.

Respectfully,
Arturo

"I came close once. He was Brazilian."

The surprised look on Angela's face gave CJ a touch of satisfaction. She liked cracking the stereotype of the middle-aged English teacher with no social life who lived with her aging parents.

"Cultural differences, huh?" Angela nodded as if she already knew the whole story.

CJ said nothing to contradict this impression. "Yeah, something like that." She pointed at the pile of essays on Angela's desk. "Are those *Romeo and Juliet* essays?"

Angela sighed. "Yeah, they're terrible."

"Maybe it's time to walk away from them for a while. That usually helps me."

Angela took CJ's advice and packed the essays into a tote bag, leaving CJ the privacy she craved to check in with Ray. Her attraction to Ray had begun with a simple gesture of understanding. She had posted her first stab at poetry—a satire of e.e. cummings—on the online class bulletin board. An uncomfortable virtual silence followed, and CJ felt a twinge of embarrassment every time she logged into the class to find no one had responded to her poem. Then Ray's four sweet words, "This cracked me up!" It was almost as if she could hear the others in the class say, "Ah, now I get it. How did I miss it?" The ice had been broken with her classmates thanks to Ray's insight and humor. It wasn't long before they started a side conversation.

RE: Poetry First Lines
FROM: CJ Dowling
DATE: Sept 15, 2007, 3:45 pm

Hi Ray,
I'd love to take you up on your offer to exchange first lines to get a poem started. When left to myself, I seem to write the same poem over and over. So here's your first line: My toes grip the rocks…
What have you got for me?
Poetically yours,
CJ

RE: Poetry First Lines
FROM: Ray Gunderson
DATE: Sept 15, 2007, 6:15 pm
TO: CJ Dowling

Hi CJ,
You're the only one who responded, so let's just do this through email (ray.gunderson@abblabs.com) rather than on the class bulletin board. Here's your line: A small scrap of silk…
Good luck! Verses 'R' Us, Ray

Since then, they had been exchanging poetry, some of it good, most of it not.

Many of Ray's poems were funny, but along the way, he also wrote some that took CJ's breath away. Her attraction for him grew steadily, mostly without her notice, until she found herself getting annoyed with Angela and saying snitty things to get her to leave school earlier each day, so she could get online and see what Ray had left for her.

Computer chimes
starts my heart
pounding
Get mail, I command
Hold my breath
hope you're there
Constant as a star, solid as granite
Your words wait
to open me up

peel me like an artichoke
petal by tough petal
until you uncover my tender, juicy
heart
ready for you to take a bite

The loud coffee machine startles her. A man finally enters the café but he's accompanied by a woman, both in business attire and obviously continuing a conversation that started before they came in. The laptop woman sighs loudly and snaps it shut. CJ watches absently as she throws away her coffee cup and a perfectly good muffin before she pulls on her jacket and packs up to leave.

CJ checks her watch: 4:03. I should follow her lead. If he's not here by now, he's not coming. She looks at her doodles all over the printed email, a series of chains, figure 8's going down the page, each string getting less and less uniform than the one before until the last one looks like a piece of yarn that has become unraveled. Her last swallow of coffee is cold and bitter. A black sludge covers the bottom of her cup.

She jots a note on the back of the email. In case there has been a mistake, she doesn't want to appear to be the one standing someone up: *Ray, I was here from 3-4, but had to go. Hope everything's okay. Did we get our wires crossed? CJ.* She leaves the note with the girl behind the counter. "Just in case a man comes in here looking for CJ." She wonders if the girl will read the note after she has left. Embarrassed and disappointed, she realizes she doesn't even care.

Back at school, she lets herself into the darkened English office, doesn't bother with the light. The red glow of the exit sign in the hall is enough. She powers on the computer and logs into her account. The mail icon taunts her. She clicks on it and sees Ray's name. The email was sent at 2:45. Her breath is shallow and quick. Where had he been at 2:45 and why was he emailing her when he was supposed to be on his way to the café? She wants to open the message but is afraid of what she might find. Her phone sits where she left it. "2 Missed Calls." She checks the times: 3:57 and 3:58. She doesn't need to check the number to know it will be Ray's. He didn't leave a message, but she feels a measure of relief anyway. He tried to contact her.

She opens his first email.

SUBJECT: I'm Here
FROM: Ray Gunderson ray.gunderson@abblabs.com
DATE: November 29, 2007, 2:45:06 PM, CDT
TO: CJ Dowling cj.dowling@geths.lcus.edu

Dear CJ,
In case you haven't left yet, I thought I'd let you know I'm here early. Can't wait to finally meet you! – R

SUBJECT: Where are you?
FROM: Ray Gunderson ray.gunderson@abblabs.com
DATE: November 29, 2007, 3:59:17 PM, CDT
TO: CJ Dowling cj.dowling@geths.lcus.edu

CJ,

I don't know what to say. A woman on your voicemail? I tried it twice. Please tell me you gave me the wrong number. – R

SUBJECT: Leaving
FROM: Ray Gunderson ray.gunderson@abblabs.com
DATE: November 29, 2007, 4:05:17 PM, CDT
TO: CJ Dowling cj.dowling@geths.lcus.edu

I wait
Coffee's comfort, now tart
Feeling stupid
I left

CJ doesn't know what to make of the series of emails. Why wouldn't she have a woman's voice on her voice mail? If Ray was at the coffee shop all that time, where was he? Was there another room she hadn't noticed? A nook back by the bathrooms where Ray had been all along, calling her and emailing her while she sat across the room from him? Or was this some kind of sick joke?

CJ can't express it in a full thought, but she senses a glimmer of understanding even before her training in logic starts to kick in. Why *not* a woman's voice? Because Ray was expecting a *man's* voice? Had CJ ever said anything to indicate she was a man? Of course, it wouldn't be the first time someone assumed she was male from her name, but surely her gender was clear from their email conversations. She combed her brain trying to think. Even if she hadn't told him she was a woman,

Ray never said anything to indicate he was gay. Wouldn't that be something you'd want to establish for sure before meeting a stranger with whom you'd exchanged poetry?

Then she realizes all the un-filled blanks she left before she agreed to meet Ray. Hell, she didn't even do an Internet search—something as simple as punching in his first and last name and maybe "Abbot Labs" just to see if he really did exist and was who he said he was. That would have taken minutes, less than a minute.

"ray gunderson + abbott labs" she types in the search box. She stops before pushing the search button. She isn't sure what she is afraid of but hesitates nonetheless. She takes off her jacket.

"Search."

The first few hits listed don't look like what she is looking for, but halfway down the screen, she finds it. She clicks on the link and finds the bio and picture for Ray Gunderson, Senior Researcher. Instead of the handsome face she imagined when she read his poetry, a formal portrait of a middle-aged woman looks at her. The woman wears a violet business suit with a colorful scarf draped gracefully around her neck.

She toggles back to Ray's email. "In case you haven't left yet. I'm here…" CJ closes her eyes and tries to remember the woman, her sister in being stood up, at the coffee shop. The hair could be hers although she wears it a bit shorter in the photo. Then CJ's eye catches the email address at the end of the biographical material: ray.gunderson@abblabs.com.

CJ logs into the class website and searches for the self-introductions that people posted at the beginning of the course. There is Ray's. CJ had glanced through the bios briefly and surely must have missed something that indicated a gender for Ray. There it is under *Random Fact About Me*: "I was named after a beloved great uncle though why my parents didn't choose to spell my name 'Rae', I have no idea. It's caused no end of confusion my whole life."

You don't know the half of it.

She goes back through the email exchanges looking for clues, but once she knows Ray is a woman, everything becomes obvious to her. How could she have ever thought otherwise? She opens the folder where she saved Ray's poetry. There blinking on the screen are metaphors and images that made her fall in love with Ray, or the man she thought Ray was. Over twenty years since she has felt this way, over twenty years since Arturo broke her heart. She lets out a laugh. This would be a great example for her unit on irony, though her students would probably wonder what the big deal was.

CJ remembers her college friend, Mary, telling her about another female student who had come on to her at a party. Mary seemed so repulsed by the whole thing that CJ mirrored her feelings of disgust. In truth, though, she simply saw the situation as a case of miscommunication. Last she heard, Mary had been in a relationship with a woman for over twenty-five years. Sometimes people hide things even from themselves.

She toggles back to Ray's picture and imagines what she is doing right now, feeling stood up, just like CJ did, maybe drinking a glass of wine. Could they end up being friends? Something more? CJ isn't exactly at the time in life where you "change teams" as the kids would say, but then she also doesn't mind taking a swipe at stereotypes from time to time either. She picks up her cell phone then stops. She flips it closed and opens a new document on the desktop. Poetry has gotten them into this and poetry will have to get them out.

Deer Camp

Yeah, we were drunker'n skunks. Yeah, we smoked some weed. Yeah, we were at Jamie's step-ma's brother's hunting cabin outside of Antigo. Yeah, we done a lot of crazy things at deer camp before. But mostly just trips to the strip club south of Elmhurst

This year, Jamie was pissier than usual, which surprised me. I figured with his old man gone, Jamie'd lighten up a little. I mean, if it was me, I'da been glad *not* to have my dad there calling me a pussy, saying if I was more of a man I'd shoot a damn deer. Up until now, we cut Jamie some slack. All except Smitty who liked to stir things up.

"Hey." Smitty downed a shot and grabbed the black garbage bag he left next to the shelf of old videos. He looked straight at Jamie pouting in the plaid chair in the corner and opened the bag. He used a fake girl voice.

"Whaddya say, boys?" He pulled out an armful of big old-lady dresses, a bunch of high-heel shoes and a pouch full of makeup. You coulda heard a pin drop. Jamie leaned forward and put his elbows on his knees, but he didn't say nothing, just stared two holes straight through Smitty's chest.

Smitty grinned and fluffed out a flowery dress, held it up in front of him, batted his eyes at Jamie.

Me and Will looked over at Jamie who leaned back and downed the rest of his Bud. I don't think he even had to swallow; he just poured it straight down his throat. He put the empty can on the end table next to him. His nostrils flared as he took a big breath. I held mine. Then he got the shit-eatin'est grin on his face I ever seen. Musta been the pot. He stood up, grabbed a blue striped bundle outta Smitty's hand and dropped trow. It was like the whole room let out a breath.

"Atta girl!" Smitty laughed. He balled up a yellow and green thing and tossed it at me.

"Where the hell?" I threw it back at him.

"Cleaned out my aunt's house last weekend." He flung it at me again, almost knocking over my beer.

"Fat Aunt Trudy," Will giggled. "Gimme one." Pretty soon, he was wobbling around on a pair of shiny black heels. Slips and nylons came out of nowhere, even a pack of Virginia Slims. Smitty kept pulling out stuff. I put on some blue eye shadow, and Jamie smeared his mouth with Sierra Sunset lipstick. We cracked up at the name, lisping all the s's. Smitty opened up another bottle of Beam, poured some in one of Aunt Trudy's shoes and we passed it around. "Drink! Drink! Drink!" Jamie grabbed the shoe and downed it with his fist up in the air, his big hairy armpit hanging out of the sleeveless dress. I laughed so hard I almost wet my panty hose.

Someone said, "Man, good thing no one's taking pictures of this." I think it was me. Jamie growled, "Put that damn thing away, you asshole." He made a grab for

Smitty's disposable camera, threatening to flush it down the toilet. I blacked out before I could find out if he did.

Next morning, we slept through the alarm, all except Jamie. He was up and out already. The rest of us were pulling on our wool pants, when we heard the report of his rifle. We looked at each other. Waited for a second shot.

"One shot is what it's all about," we said together like Robert DeNiro in *The Deer Hunter*. Then, as if we all remembered Jamie's old man at the same time, we put on the faces we wore at the funeral and got real interested in tying our boots.

We put on our blaze orange and headed out to help Jamie gut his deer and drag it back to the cabin.

Looking for a blood trail, we spiraled out from Jamie's tree stand. Nothing. "Maybe we should yell?" Second time anybody'd said anything all morning.

"Nah. We'll find him." Not good to piss off other hunters within earshot. I did a slow 360 and saw Jamie's orange jacket and hat a couple hundred yards off.

When we got to him, he was standing over the doe. Her legs were still twitching, and her eyes were rolling around like she'd gone crazy. The sound that came from her was like a sob. I was about to say, "What the hell's the matter with you? Kill her for god's sake." But then I saw Jamie's eyes. They were red with two black streaks running down his cheeks. A smear of Sierra Sunset like a clown mouth.

Smitty took the rifle from his loose grip, stepped between him and the deer. The only thing on Jamie that moved were his eyelids. He shut them so tight I thought his face would fold in on itself. Smitty put the barrel of the gun between the animal's crazy eyes and pulled the trigger.

How to Play with Fire

When You're About to Play with Fire

Shift into Park. Take off your wedding ring. Put it in the cup holder next to the gearshift and slide your empty water bottle over it. Not that someone looking for valuables to steal would notice the thin gold band and diamond-chip engagement ring. Not that anyone would expect anything of value in a ten-year-old Kia in the parking lot of a tired, half-occupied office building on a Friday morning anyway.

The irony of this small action is not lost on you: hiding your wedding ring to protect it from being stolen at the same time you're about to break your vow. But you must get that ring off your hand. Now. Before you lose your nerve.

Turn off the engine and pay attention to what you do with the keys after you take them out of the ignition. Talk about an afterglow killer, having to call your husband to rescue you when you realize you've locked your keys in the car. After your only extramarital encounter in seven years of marriage. Would that be a cliché or irony? You don't want to find out.

Slip the keys into the outside pocket of your purse. Fish your phone from the crack between the passenger seat and gearshift console. Try to ignore the text from Patrick. Pretend not to notice the "X" and the "O" after he tells you he'll pick up Macey from daycare. Try not to feel like a major bitch for translating this message as *An extra half-hour with Alex in your office*. Alone.

Do stop for a moment to enjoy the sensation of warmth and moisture, the slight change in your breathing when you think about Alex.

When You're About to Be Magnanimous
Make it seem like something that just occurred to you. "You know, Meg, there's no reason you have to wait around here until four." Your assistant's desk is clear. You can't see her computer screen, but you're pretty sure she's playing solitaire to pass the time. You haven't picked up enough clients to justify her salary anyway. So much for Patrick's brilliant idea to leave New York and open your own freelance editing business here in Milwaukee, of all places. "You must have a million things to get done before the rehearsal dinner."

Meg looks grateful.

"Really? You don't mind?"

"Of course not. As far as I'm concerned, the mother of the bride shouldn't work at all on the day before her daughter's wedding." Smile. "Go."

She thanks you, extracts her purse from her bottom drawer and checks your schedule.

"Looks like you've only got a one o'clock with Alex. Quiet afternoon."

When Doubt Seeps In
Review the list of signs.

1. How a flush rises in his cheeks when you look him straight in the eye and compliment his writing.

2. How he takes extra sips of water when you sit side by side at the work table, then ends up with hiccups and you now share an inside joke.

3. How he's stopped referring to his wife. In fact, it has been so long that you've forgotten her name, if you ever knew it at all. Okay, that's not true. You met her at the launch party, but you have completely obliterated her name from your memory. Lisa, maybe.

4. How he's stopped asking about your husband and daughter and focuses exclusively on questions whose answers he already knows. Questions about your travels before you met Patrick, before Macey came along. As if keeping you mentally in that time prevents them from existing. And how happily you stay in that period. "You were in Bangkok, right? What year was that again?" As if willing your visits to coincide. Perhaps you'd eaten in the same restaurant. Maybe he'd bought you a drink and you'd gone to the night market together. But, of course, his Peace Corps stint had ended long before your six-week homestay during high school.

When Guilt Pays a Visit
Remind yourself that you're not looking for anything long-term. Just a little something to make you feel like you've still got it. And, be honest, to punish Patrick just a bit. Not that he'll ever know.

Remind yourself of everything you left behind in New York. If you were there right now, you'd be having lunch at *Billy's* chatting up the Random House types and starting to make headway toward a mid-level editor position. Instead, in a moment of post-partum sentimentality, you let Patrick convince you that Macey needed a backyard and grandparents nearby.

Remember the look on Samantha's face when you broke the news over drinks after work. "Milwaukee?!" She'd almost snorted as she said it. When she realized you weren't joking, she got serious. "It's not exactly a literary hotbed, girlfriend. What about your career?"

At the time, you tamped down your thoughts that she might be right about Patrick's hometown. After all, this kind of work was something you could do from literally *anywhere.* "Bhutan or Rio," you told her.

"Well, for God's sake, go to Bhutan or Rio, then." She finished her drink. "At least they're exotic. Don't go to Milwaukee."

You feel a certain regret now as you realize how right she was. The only clients you've been able to pick up are one step above the vanity publishing crowd. So much for Patrick's assurance you'd get plenty of work in Milwaukee. It's as if the publishing world thinks you fell off the face of the planet when you moved from New York. In many ways, that's true.

When He Arrives

Look at your watch pretending you can't believe it's one o'clock already and time for your appointment. Give him a warm smile.

Today it will be chapters nine through twelve, the weakest so far. What you should say early in the consult is, *These chapters really need to go*. But that would kill the mood, so you decide you'll begin by pointing out the elements that are working, a detail here, a turn of phrase there.

Close your laptop. Push your chair back from the desk. In the doorway, he's wearing his kid grin, a combination of admiration and gratitude. In the beginning, he couldn't stop thanking you for taking him on. Truth is, the manuscript for his first book, *Out There*, was a first-class mess, worse than this one in many ways. Still, it was full of potential, and, in those days, you had the balls to be tough on him.

As you spent hours together over the final edits, you sensed a third party in the room—attraction. You're not quite sure where it came from. In a bar, you'd dismiss the gray at his temples, his thick glasses. Maybe it's the way he laps up your suggestions for revisions. Maybe you've fallen in love with the younger, more adventurous Alex of his book, who backpacked across Southeast Asia before he met his wife.

At your final editing session, you suggested a second book. "That'll be the next question, you know: What are you working on now?" You leaned forward a little. "It's the kiss of death not to have an answer."

He looked grave and told you about a draft of a love story he had on an old floppy disk somewhere. You knew *Out There* would have some legs in the small press world and you could probably whip a second Alex Chandler book into good enough shape to get some notice. "Tell you what," you lightly touched his forearm as you said it, "make it an adventure-travel-love story and we're in business."

He would have to rewrite from scratch since neither of you could find a way to access the files. You didn't say that anything written before *Out There* would surely have the mark of amateur written all over it anyway. He outlined the plot for you, trite as could be. You resisted the urge to ask him just how old he'd been when he'd written it. The way his eyes shone as he talked about Matt and Paula and how they'd spent years in dying marriages before finally finding each other, it was obvious he believed something like that could really happen. Of course, you didn't fall in love with the story, but you did start to feel a certain magnetism to the man, old-fashioned and romantic enough to believe readers would buy it.

When he described the climax, you didn't point out to him that he'd accidentally used your name in place of Paula's, but now you kind of wish you had. You might even be in bed together now instead of him taking a seat on the other side of your desk.

You'll have to change that, get him onto the couch.

He's pushing the manuscript across your desk. Another of his old-fashioned ways—he doesn't email rewrites, says he wants to be sitting in the room watching your reactions as you read. With the first book, you were able to block out his presence and go at it with red ink. As if he'd disappeared from the room completely, you'd settle into his words. But this one, it has been like a stage performance, peppering your reactions with little chuckles, an "ahh" here and there.

When you ask, he tells you the revising has been tough this week. But his eyes don't meet yours as he says it, and you don't want to go down the rewriting-is-hell-high-way, so you flick the blinker and steer the conversation another direction.

"Tell you what. Let's try something different today." You head toward the couch, stopping to pull two bottles of water from the mini-fridge on the way. "I remember I had some issues with the dialogue last time, and, since we're at the climax, it's pretty important to get that right." Sit down and pat the cushion next to you. "Why don't we read Chapter Nine aloud and see if the dialogue feels more natural this time around."

When He Sits Down
Breathe in the scent of his deodorant. Warm and spicy, it reminds you of tea shops and temples. Open his water bottle, making sure your hand brushes his as you give it to him. Don't allow it to linger so long that you're being obvious. He's wearing a soft- looking cotton shirt. Resist the urge to touch it.

"I wish I would have known." He opens the fat binder holding his rewrite. "I could have brought an extra copy."

You could make copies on the machine next to Meg's desk easily enough.

Instead, you slide closer to him. "That's okay. We can work from the same script. Why don't you read all the narration and Matt's dialogue. I'll make notes along the way and be Paula."

At first, you mark a couple things that jump out at you—wordy sentences, a point-of-view slip—making sure to balance them out with plus signs and smiley faces. Despite yourself, you are falling into the writing. Unlike in the last version, Matt sounds like a flesh-and-blood guy who really is struggling between his sense of duty to an anemic marriage and his attraction to Paula. And Paula's quest has shifted from pure sex to something deeper.

"Laura has pancreatic cancer." Alex's voice has the same inflection he uses when reading Matt's dialogue, but these words aren't on the page. Comb your brain to figure out who Laura is, and then it comes to you. His wife.

Pancreatic isn't one of those you nail with chemo and get five more good years. A selfish glimmer, which you don't even allow to become a full thought, streaks through your mind. Stare straight ahead trying to think of the right thing to say. Realize he's been holding this news since he walked through the door, as you lured him to the couch, snuggled up next to him to read. If you were to let yourself, you'd be able to recognize the signs of his worry from the moment he poked his head into your office. But you don't.

Unable to think of the right words, you say, "Oh, Alex, I'm sorry—" Let your face ask the questions he's going to answer anyway.

He takes off his glasses. His eyes are dry and clear. "We found out Monday. Stage four. They're talking months, not years." Instead of a voice choked with grief or fear, which you'd expect, his is matter-of-fact. "She's decided not to do anything. Chemo, I mean. There's no surgery." A grimace plays at his lips. "Ironic, huh?"

Quell the urge to point out that this would be a misuse of the term, but you can see the ironic nature of the situation. "Yeah, that must have been a tough call." Consider the calendar. In all likelihood, she'll be gone by Christmas. Finally, you find something appropriate to say.

"How are you doing with—everything?"

"Oh, God. I don't know. I mean I'm probably *supposed* to want her to fight it," he says. "Even though I've thought about leaving a hundred times once the kids went to college, it's not like I want her to be," he pauses, "dead."

Mirror his shaking head. Of course, you'd never think he'd wish his wife dead.

"But, well, do you want me to be honest?"

At first you think he is asking just to make sure you're listening, but he stops and waits for an answer like he really wants to know. You, on the other hand, aren't so sure you want him to be honest. You can't very well say that, of course. "Sure, you can tell me," because you do like the *idea* of him confiding in you.

"To be honest, she has been nothing but angry for the past ten years. I think she blames me for her unhappiness or something."

Nod.

"Maybe it is my fault. Who knows? The more I think about it, it's almost like the cancer will put us both out of her misery." He looks at his hands, cleans his glasses with a cloth from his front shirt pocket, rests the glasses back on the coffee table. "That's awful, isn't it?"

You realize you've been clenching your jaw, trying not to see this from Laura's point of view.

"No, not awful," you say. "Just human."

His face relaxes. Take a drink from your water bottle, so you don't have to look at him. You hope for a sob or a tear or something when he speaks again, but his voice is solid. "Okay then, while I'm being *human*, I have a confession to make." His body is so close to yours now you can feel his soft shirt on your forearm and swear you can sense the heat radiating from his groin. What you would have given for this just a few minutes ago. He reaches for your left hand, notices your missing ring, smiles. His goatee tickles your palm as he kisses it. He breathes in deeply as if he's trying to take in the entirety of your aroma. Because it is the only thing you can do, close your eyes.

When You're About to Get Something You Thought You Wanted But Now Aren't So Sure
Keep your eyes closed.

That's what you tell Macey to do when something scares her. Close your eyes, and, when you open them again, everything will look different.Remind yourself that this is exactly what you wanted. Remind yourself of the list and the fact that it has been months since Patrick has tried to initiate lovemaking. Months since you've felt his breath on your neck, since his tongue has visited that spot near your collarbone, the one that always puts you one flutter away from orgasm.

Yes. Right there.

Tell yourself this has nothing to do with Alex's dying wife, that he's been waiting to kiss you like this since before his wife got sick, that his kisses aren't a desperate attempt to assuage his guilt about his relief that she'll be gone. That it's you he's attracted to.

Open your eyes.

When You Drive Home
Try to shake the image of his disappointed face from your mind. Turn up the radio. Switch channels to the headbanging station so there's no danger of some sort of *meaningful* song coming on and messing with your head. Banish all glimmers of realization that should have occurred to you as you removed your wedding ring this morning. The ring. Rescue it from under the water bottle and tell yourself nothing is different. Remind yourself how much your husband loves you. Reassure yourself that if you were to take ill, he would *not* see your diagnosis as a misery-ender. Yours or his. When you get home, he'll be cooking dinner with your daughter happily eating Cheerios in her high chair. Completely ignorant of what you almost threw away, he'll give you a peck on the cheek as you drop your briefcase on the counter and kick off your shoes.

You'll be faithful to them both from now on.

Try to convince yourself: No harm. No foul.

Open Book

Alistair and I do our homework at the island in the kitchen while, at the stove, Mom stirs Pasta Fazool. The smell of onions and garlic makes my stomach growl and almost tricks me into thinking things can be the same as they were before Mom lost her job three months ago and started going to see Mel-the-reiki-guru.

The door from the garage swings open. "Make way!" Dad is carrying two giant bags from *Flanners'*. He's wearing what Mom calls "that kid-in-a-candy-store-look." It usually precedes news about an impulsive purchase that will lead to under-their-breath arguments about credit card penalties and living within our means. Alistair and I push aside our books and calculators to make room.

Mom sighs and turns down the burner. She gives dinner one last stir before putting on the cover.

I look at Alistair and mouth, "Here we go again."

He replies with a grin that says, "Who cares?" and slides his notebooks into his backpack.

Dad pulls boxes out of the bags. "I had the world's best idea today..."

Oh, no.

"We're going to make the first *real* reality TV show."
He opens a box with a picture of what looks like a book
light on it. "Micro-cameras." He pulls out a gadget. "This
one is so small I can put it in a plant, and no one'll even
know it's there."

Cameras. This shouldn't surprise me. We spent our
early years with the eye of Dad's camcorder in our faces
and recent ones with a phone pointed our way. He titles
all his videos *The Smiths Go to...* followed by the vacation
destination. Sometimes I think he enjoys embarrassing
us by showing them to the relatives every Thanksgiving.
I have had enough with Dad's cameras, and I tell him so.

He doesn't listen. "We'll never really know *when* we're
being filmed. Eventually, we'll forget about the cameras
and start acting natural. No network, no crew. Real."

Open Book, he wants to call it. "You guys put everything
on social media sites anyway. How is this any different?"

"Well, for one thing, we're posting it ourselves," I point
out. "Someone else isn't secretly filming us." His expression tells me he doesn't see the difference.

Later that night, we complain to Mom, but she just
takes a few cleansing breaths and says, "I am giving you
a gift by not interceding here. Your relationship with
your father will be stronger for it." This is how she talks
since she started seeing Mel.

I'm tempted to say, "What about *your* relationship?"
but her expression is so peaceful I stop myself. It looks
like Alistair and I will have to derail the project ourselves.
We decide on sabotage as our first line of defense.

At first, we talk directly to the cameras, trying to taint
any appearance of "reality." We enunciate extra clearly.

"Hel-lo, Alis-tair. What is that you are having for a snack this afternoon?"

"Why, Corrine, I am having some goldfish crackers. Would you like some?"

"Oh, no, thank you. I think a banana would be more to my liking." The more artificial and boring the better.

One night, Mom apparently forgets herself and follows our lead. She threatens to serve Ginger-a-la-king. We feign horror that she is going to kill our golden retriever, Ginger, and serve her in a light gravy.

That night, Ginger gets her own chair at the dinner table. She eats off Grandma Harrington's bone china, while Alistair pretends to be Ginger narrating her day: "I was going to settle in the middle of the living room to lick my butt, but there's a camera in there, so I went to the laundry room. I figured, who would want to watch someone doing laundry? That *must* be a dummy camera, so I went in there. It sure felt good to have some privacy for a change. Gwen, could I get a little more chicken? This is delicious!"

Later, we joke about Dad's camera picking up footage of Ginger throwing up her dinner all over the family room couch. Dad smiles. "Even the fake stuff is real, you know."

After a few days, I sneak into Dad's study and find his password list under the folder in his desk drawer and log in on his computer to see what he has gotten so far. I find the *Open Book* file. It contains a bunch of clips of the most boring stuff imaginable: Mom filling the washing machine, Alistair playing video games, Ginger sleeping in the hallway. There's no way any of this will become one of Dad's film projects.

Then, in the last folder, I see a shot of my bedroom doorway, from inside the room. Alistair walks in, closes the door behind him and goes directly to my underwear drawer, where I keep my dummy journal. I know he's been sneaking into my room to read it for years. He disappears from the frame to sit on my bed while he reads the last entry I wrote, completely fictional, about spying on him and Madeline Engleberger kissing behind the equipment shed by the tennis courts at school.

Then I realize what I'm looking at: film footage taken without my knowledge, in my bedroom. My *bedroom*. I try to remember everything I've done in my room that would have been in the camera's view. Every morning, I dress in the bathroom after my shower. At night, I change into my pajamas near the hamper in my closet. That's way off screen. In total, the camera can see the edge of my dresser and the door. I wonder what Dad thinks he is going to catch from that angle. This time he caught a kid reading his sister's diary. It's not much, but he obviously thought it was important enough to save.

I search through computer files for other footage, but all I can find are the old *The Smiths Go to...* videos labeled by location and year. I close out the windows I opened and slide the folder back over his passwords.

In my room, I stand in my doorway and try to see the camera in the ceiling fan. He's hidden it expertly but not completely. I stand on my bed and reach up to rip the thing down, then think again. Dad's a teacher. He's all about learning. Maybe I can teach him something.

At the end of the school day on Monday, I slide up behind Jack and put my hands over his eyes. "Guess who?" We have been best friends since preschool, so I can do this sort of thing without any rumors starting about us hooking up.

"Why, Manny, what soft hands you have," he says, pretending I'm his locker neighbor. Not everyone knows Jack has a sense of humor.

"Very funny. I need your help."

On the way home, I tell him about Dad's project. Jack, a believer in the benefit of the doubt, offers reasons Dad might put a camera in my room. "You said yourself, he had it focused on your door. Maybe he's going to speed up the film and show you coming and going out of your room, like bees in a hive."

"Seriously?"

He shrugs. "Well, at least you said the camera can't really *see* anything."

"Yup, it's what the camera *can't* see that will make our footage interesting." I fill him in on my plan.

When we get to my house, I let us in through the garage door and grab a baseball cap hanging on a peg. "Put this on." I don't want Dad to recognize him.

We drop our bags and head upstairs. I open my bedroom door and act like I'm sneaking him in. I close the door behind him. "Keep your head down," I whisper as I put one hand on each shoulder and try to make it look like I'm kissing him.

Pretending to take off my shirt, I walk toward my bed, which is outside the camera's view. When I turn around, Jack almost runs right up my back. We sit on the bed trying not to bust out laughing. I don't *think* there's a mic in here but I can't be sure.

We shift our weight to make the bedsprings squeak. He tries to hold in his chuckle but ends up letting out a snort, which makes me laugh. I try to turn it into a moan like in movie sex scenes.

I am tempted to purr, "Oh, God!" but know that if I try to make words, I won't be able to keep from laughing. We sit back-to-back to get ourselves under control. When we're breathing normally again, I check my watch. We've been here exactly two minutes. On our way home, we decided we should take at least twenty minutes to make our "encounter" seem real. I show Jack my watch. His face says what I'm thinking: what are we going to do for eighteen more minutes?

We lie on our backs with our legs dangling over the side of the bed and stare at the ceiling. I let my eyes follow a crack in the plaster from the light fixture to my closet door and back again. I count how many clock ticks it takes for each of Jack's breaths. Four in. Four out. I close my eyes and think about how lucky I am to have a friend like Jack. Who else could I tell about Dad's crazy project much less talk into a pretend sex scene?

Before I know it, my body feels like it's in a free-fall, and I land on my bed with a jerk. I feel like I've been asleep for an hour, but it has been only five minutes since the last time I checked my watch. Long enough.

Jack's eyes are closed, but it doesn't seem like he's sleeping. I nudge him and point to my watch. "Let's go," I mouth. He gives me a thumbs-up. He puts the cap back on his head and pulls it extra low. I wish I could see Dad's face when he watches this footage. We stop at the door for one final pretend kiss.

Downstairs, we find Jack's backpack, and I put the cap back on its hook. "Hey. Thanks again. I'll let you know how it turns out." As I close the door behind him, I notice the camera on top of the fridge is missing. I look for the one next to the picture on the mantle. Gone. I run up to my room knowing what I'll find before I get there. The camera is nowhere to be seen. I've acted out a pretend sex scene with my best friend for nothing.

Cameras appear in different places then disappear again. We never do forget about them like Dad hoped we would, but we do seem to stop caring about what they might catch while we're living our "real" lives. In fact, I use every opportunity I can to let Dad in on things I want him to know but would never tell him to his face. I tell him how I miss the time right after dinner when he used to rebound my free throws in the driveway while Mom and Alistair cleaned up the dishes, and how he'd make up word games to play while we hit the badminton birdie back and forth in the side yard.

One day, I talk directly to a camera planted in the basket on the kitchen counter and tell him I think he's addicted to his computer, that it's his fixation with technology—not getting laid off from her job—that led Mom to start going to Mel. Then I stop midsentence because there's no way to know if Dad actually hears any of my confessions. So far, it doesn't seem like he has. Everything is exactly the same. He disappears into his office every night right after dinner. Alistair and I get stuck doing the dishes, while Mom stretches out with her laptop on the living room couch.

Come to think of it, Mom seems to be fostering her own relationship with the computer since she started working from home as a consultant. When I walk past, she quickly opens a new window but not before I can see she is on Facebook. I settle into the chair across from her, log into my own page and search for her hyphenated last name, "Harrington-Smith." No dice. Maybe her account is under plain "Harrington." Nope. I know it would be worthless to search for her using Smith. Finally, reasoning that all mothers want access to their daughter's Facebook world, I ask her if she wants to be Friends.

"That's sweet dear. But we really need to have our own," she searches for the word, "circles." At first, I think she's kidding, but she isn't. "You need privacy from me, and…" She doesn't need to finish. My own mother rejected my Facebook Friend request. In person. I wonder if she did the same thing to Dad and that's why he moved on to his reality TV project.

Now I can't sleep. I've tried lying on my right side, on my left, then on my back again. I flip over my pillow hoping the other side is cooler. I decide to get a cool washcloth and a drink of water.

On the carpet runner, my footsteps are so quiet I can hear the tap of fingers on a keyboard alternating with mouse clicks. The clicking stops. I peek through the half-open door of Dad's study and realize he has in earbuds. His t-shirt hangs over the arm of his chair. It's weird to see him sitting at his desk in no shirt and his sleep shorts. Even though the fan blows straight at him, he needs to wipe the sweat off his face and the back of his neck with his t-shirt. From this vantage, it looks like he's editing video. I stretch my neck to try to see what it is even though I sense I really don't want to know.

He leans back giving me a full view of the screen. At first, I don't know what I'm looking at. Girls who seem to be my age are strutting around in school uniforms, dark blue and red plaid skirts, knee socks and navy blazers with an emblem on the left front pocket. I immediately think of the private school in Lake Mills but their uniforms are forest green and maroon. These girls look like they're trying to seduce the cameraman.

The frame zooms in on a blonde girl running her tongue over her shiny, red lower lip. I clench my jaws together and breathe through my nose like Mom tells me to when I am sick to my stomach. The blonde leans over to show her cleavage, squeezes her breasts together like she's offering them up as an appetizer. I close my eyes, wanting to run straight back to my room. Instead, I am paralyzed, a line of sweat running slowly down my spine. By the time I open my eyes, Dad's body is blocking the screen again. I go back to my room without the washcloth or the drink of water.

When I finally go downstairs the next day, my eyes feel like someone has gone at them with a piece of sandpaper. My skin feels like it's covered with a sticky film. Dad is eating a sandwich at the island in the kitchen tapping on his phone. He looks like he always does—so much so that I start to think maybe I imagined the whole perverted thing. But then he picks up his napkin and wipes sweat from the back of his neck, just like he did last night.

Dad is always telling us we can talk to him about anything, especially the important things, and I can't see anything more important than what's happening in this house right now.

"Dad, can we talk?" I have no idea what I'm going to say, only that I need to say something.

He holds up one finger and keeps scrolling and tapping the screen. I know he thinks only a few seconds have passed, but, when the silence lasts into the second minute, I remind him I'm here. "Dad?"

"What? Oh, yeah. Okay." He makes one more swipe of his finger and three more taps, puts his phone on the counter next to him, face up, takes another bite of sandwich and talks with a full mouth. "What's up?"

I don't know how to come right out and say, "I know you're watching and maybe even filming porn movies. School girl porn. It's disgusting, so stop." But I don't get a chance to go any further because his phone buzzes.

His eyes jerk to the screen to check out the number even though he keeps his face pointed at me. "It's not important." He pushes the phone two inches to the right as if it really doesn't matter. "I'll call them back later. Now, where were we?" The phone buzzes once more to tell him he has a missed call and then one more time to show a text is coming in.

"Forget it." I open the refrigerator and look inside. "It's nothing."

"Corrine?"

I know he won't leave me alone until I say *something*, so I say, "I was just wondering when I could get a new phone. I think mine's dying."

"Sure thing." He smiles as he picks up his phone. He's swiping and tapping again. "It'll have to be next Saturday though. Your mother and I have a wedding to go to this afternoon." I realize I'll have to find a different way to let him know what's on my mind.

I pour Fruit Loops into a bowl and head back up to my room. After I finish eating, I doodle awhile and then stare at the David Beckham poster over my desk. Every time my thoughts go back to the image of the girl in the school uniform, I try to imagine explanations for what I saw last night. Maybe he didn't film that footage at all. Maybe he's doing research on Internet porn or looking for clips to splice into a documentary about human trafficking. A group in my social studies class did a project on it for their final exam. Horrible. I hope extra hard that this is the real explanation. Deep down, I know it's not.

I send Jack a text: *Tell me again my dad isn't a perv.* His phone must be off because he doesn't answer.

I spend the rest of the day trying to think of what to do. I consider going to Mom but can't imagine what I would say. I start to write each of them a letter, but when I try to put this whole mess into words, I sound like an overdramatic teenager on a stupid sitcom.

By the time they leave for the wedding, I decide to talk to my dad in his own language. This time, I'm going to get it right.

I walk down the hall to his office and wiggle the mouse to wake up his computer. I log in and start sifting through his video clips trying to find the footage I saw last night. Like a detective getting into the head of a perp, I ask myself what he would do to cover his tracks. It occurs to me he might disguise his dirty-movie files as *The Smiths Go to...* videos, but those turn out to be exactly what their titles say they are.

I decide to check Dad's Internet history, hoping there's nothing resembling an online porn site, that I dreamed the whole sordid situation. But there it is: sexyschoolgirls.com. At the place in the video where I closed my eyes, the girl sits on the teacher's desk and pulls up her knees and spreads them apart. No underwear. Disgusting. I click the pause button. The filmmaking doesn't look like Dad's usual work. This was filmed on equipment far more advanced than Dad has. At least the equipment I know about.

Alistair comes home from his soccer tournament. I put the computer into sleep mode and go downstairs to see how it went. He takes a container of yogurt and bag of chips into his room. With Mom and Dad gone, he'll play video games until he falls asleep or our parents come home, whichever comes first.

Back in Dad's office, I make use of all skills I learned making film projects for social studies through the years. I copy and cut video clips from his projects, then record a scene from sexyschoolgirls.com using my phone. It's weird to say, but I like the gritty effect of a video of a laptop screen. Makes it feel "real."

I rearrange the scenes and add transitions, effects and background music. The result surprises me: a two-minute video that clearly sums up the past few weeks in our crazy house. I add footage of me talking directly to the camera and burn the project to a disk. I title it *Corrine's Open Book*.

Downstairs I put the disc in the DVD player and turn down the volume on the TV, so Alistair can't hear it. The video begins with footage from when I was four: *The Smiths Go to Glacier National Park*.

I have fallen off a pony and knocked out my front teeth before they are ready to come out. My mom is holding me on her lap, a blood-covered washcloth stuffed in my mouth. She's rocking me back and forth, trying to get me to stop crying. "Shh. There, there," she's saying even though her voice is drowned out by my sobbing. She's stroking my forehead and kissing my temple, but her eyes are shooting daggers at my dad behind the camera. "Put that thing away!" She shifts her body on the bench, so he has to move if he wants to continue to take the close-up of my bleeding mouth. I can't remember the last time she stood up for me like that with Dad.

The next clip I shot over my mom's shoulder with my phone when she was absorbed in an online exchange with Mel-the-reiki-master. You can't see what she's typing, but when she looks up and finds me watching her, she ends her conversation immediately and reminds me about the importance of respecting each other's privacy.

Next, the scene cuts to the shot of Alistair sneaking my journal out of my drawer.

While the camera stays on the dresser, I give a voiceover. "Dear Diary, I learned something really creepy about my dad today. When he's not splicing together film clips to embarrass the hell out of his family, he's watching porn on the Internet. Teenage girl porn."

The film switches to the classroom scene with blondie in the classroom. I cut it right after she shows her cleavage, just in case Alistair should accidentally see the DVD. He doesn't need to see anything more than *that*.

The final scene is me looking straight at the camera. "Here's what I think," I say. Even though my voice sounds confident, it is clear from the way my neck muscles clench and my eyes have a hard time settling on the camera that I really don't know what I want to say. I deliver the lines I practiced before I turned on the camera: "This is a wake up call. There's creepy stuff happening in this house and Alistair and I are too young to deal with it. Figure it out, will ya?" Even though I don't cry on the video, I have to wipe my face as I watch myself. I push the power button on the DVD player, and the room is silent again.

I walk over to the bookshelf where we keep the photo albums and turn on the light keeping the dimmer turned low. I sit on the floor with one of the albums on my lap. The book is so thick the binding creaks when I open it. Looking at photos, I don't get that nauseated feeling I get when Dad plays our travel videos. Something about the freeze-frame makes me feel like I'm not the same person as the girl in the picture who has carrot sticks poking out of her ears and an orange wedge in her smile where her teeth should be.

Then there is the photo of me wearing Mom's wedding veil. It was taken four years ago on a snow day that kept us all cooped up in the house. Mom had decided it would be a good day to clean the basement and get rid of the toys we'd outgrown. At first, we enjoyed sorting through things, but soon we all got a little restless. Mom was trying to talk Alistair into getting rid of his Kinex set when Dad turned around from sorting through the old dress up bin. A pink boa was draped around his neck. He wore bright green star-shaped sunglasses and a clown's rainbow-striped wig. "Yoo hoo," he waved the boa like he was flirting with us, his voice as high as a girl's. "What's all the fuss about?"

Pretty soon Mom was marching around with an eye patch, Mardi Gras beads, and a Happy New Year 2007 glitter-covered tiara. Alistair found a matted auburn beard at the bottom of the trunk and topped off his getup with a sparkly gypsy vest and pink high heels.

I held up a bent beaded circle with a fluff of white netting on the back. "This looks like the thing on your head in your wedding picture."

"It is." Mom set the band on my head and fiddled with the netting. "Look at that, Charlie. Isn't she beautiful?"

It was hard to take him seriously in his clown wig, but Dad's voice was sincere. "She's the spitting image of you, Gwen." He pulled her toward him. "What do you think? Would you marry this clown all over again?"

"In a heartbeat." She smiled. "Arrrr. Got a kiss for Captain Jack?"

Remembering the scene brings back the feeling I got when I was a kid and my mom and dad were kissing.

Half of me didn't want to watch because I thought it was gross. The other half wanted to linger in the moment because the kiss meant our family was solid.

I slip the picture from the album and prop it next to the DVD player and find a piece of scrap paper next to the phone. "Mom and Dad: Push Play" I draw an arrow pointing down and tape it to the TV. My hands are shaking. I guess I know that what they'll see could demolish whatever bit of family we have left. Still I can't know what I know all by myself. That's the job of the parents. I turn off all the lights except the lamp near the TV and go up to bed.

Good News

Grace could see her breath as she chanted with the other Good Newsers on the corner across the street from the clinic. "Not a choice! It's a child!" She felt a surge of pride as the voices melded into one, her soul washed clean. It felt good to yell at the top of her lungs. At strangers.

She rehoisted her sign to make the picture of the aborted baby visible to people driving past. Although the bloody image would probably visit her dreams, she knew the photograph was her strongest ammunition to persuade the women—no, *mothers*, Roger kept reminding them—persuade the *mothers* not to murder their babies. Grace had a hard time thinking of them as mothers, though. She had felt nothing like a mother when she'd experienced her own unintended pregnancy the semester before she dropped out of college and moved home.

"Not a choice!"

A rusty sedan with a Clinton-Gore bumper sticker pulled into the parking lot across the street. When the group reached its crescendo, Roger held up his hand. Their volume dropped so individuals could be heard.

"It's not too late!"

"Don't kill your baby!"

"Adoption, not abortion!"

Grace threw in, "Put it in God's hands!" before the clinic door closed.

Roger patted Grace's shoulder. "Atta girl, Gracey. We're doing the Lord's work here."

Ever since Roger had learned Grace hadn't been raised in a Christian home—her mother was an atheist, her father an unchurched Unitarian—he'd shown a special interest in Grace and her religious path. Maybe that's why he personally invited her along for the Ash Wednesday morning protest in Eau Claire. Shepherding Grace seemed to be the closest he could get to missionary work in Altoona, Wisconsin. And, since she had plenty of time on her hands, working only part-time at the library while her friends were still away at college, Grace was fine with letting Roger minister to her. Maybe he could help her understand God and his mysterious ways.

A half-hour passed with no one to yell at. The protestors huddled in twos and threes, shifting their weight from foot to foot to keep warm. Smokers found a place out of the wind and debated whether the new assistant pastor's sermons put too much emphasis on forgiveness and not enough on punishment. Grace stood next to Emily and Harriet, from the church knitting circle, the only other women in their group of twelve.

"Here comes a bus!" Emily warned.

The giant puddle would soak them all if the bus came in too close or too fast. It did both. A wave of water jumped the curb, soaking the protestors' feet. The door

opened to reveal a college-age girl looking for a dry path
out of the bus. She wore a burgundy down coat with
a faux fur collar, a smudge of ashes on her forehead.
Something in her expression made Grace think she had
come to join their protest.

Roger reached out to her. "Watch your step. That
puddle is deeper than it looks." The girl took his hand.
"On three, jump across."

She landed on the curb, found her balance and thanked
him. Her scarf, draped through her purse strap, came
loose and landed next to the puddle without her notice.
"Ma'am," Grace called, "your scarf." She made her way
around the other protestors, picked it up and started
in the direction the girl had gone, but by then she had
already crossed the street and was doubling back toward
the clinic.

"She's going for an abortion!" Emily shouted.

As if he had been personally betrayed, Roger began
to chant with extra volume. His nostrils flared. The veins
stood out on his neck. The other Good Newsers scrambled for signs and tried to meet the cadence of his words,
but they couldn't get one thing said in unison before the
doors closed behind the girl. Grace squeezed the water
out of the scarf and wrapped it around the stick that
held her sign, wondering at Roger's ability to switch so
quickly from gentleman to judge.

He closed his eyes and held up his hand.

"Let us pray."

The Good Newsers bowed their heads. Roger called
on the Lord to give them strength to continue to stand
up for babies who couldn't speak for themselves.

Grace wasn't sure why she kept the scarf. She had meant to wash and dry it, then slip it into the donation bin for the *St. Vincent de Paul.* Maybe it was the softness of the angora yarn, just a few rows of the red fluff knitted in here and there among other colors and textures. Maybe it was because Grace recognized its Harlequin pattern, the pattern the church ladies had taught her when they'd recruited her for the knitting circle. Or maybe it was the scarf's scent—a combination of Love's Baby Soft and cigarettes—that wafted into her nostrils when she wrapped it around her neck later. With each breath, Grace could hear the prayers of the girl—the *mother*, she corrected herself—asking God to end her pregnancy.

Some people didn't believe God answered prayers, but Grace was living proof He did.

Months earlier when she had missed her period the week after midterms, Grace didn't believe she could be pregnant. Since the night in Danny's dorm room, she'd convinced herself they hadn't really gone as far as they had, that he hadn't been inside her long enough to get her pregnant, that he really *did* have a lot to do now that baseball season was starting, and that he wasn't avoiding her because she was no longer a virgin. That she wasn't facing an unwanted pregnancy alone.

When four more weeks passed, she did something she had never done before: she started to pray. "Please, God, let me not be pregnant." She didn't know if she believed in God or not, but she was desperate.

A week later, her prayer changed to, "Please, God, take this baby from my womb." One more week—the fear of telling her parents pressing on her chest like a weight—she knelt on the tile floor of her dorm room as soon as her roommate had left for classes. "Take this baby. Take this baby." But her thoughts, which it turned out God could hear, too, said, "Kill this baby. Kill it."

He answered her prayer, first with a small spot of blood in her underwear and then with a whole toilet bowl full of it. She flushed away the quarter-sized clot and took to her bed. *I wished my own child dead. God answered my prayer.* She wasn't sure if that said more about her or about God, but she did know she wanted to figure it out.

Before long, the semester ended—she finished with 2 F's and 2 D's—and the decision was made for Grace to take a semester off to "get her head on straight." She moved home and spent many long days watching television and repainting her toenails until Roger and Muriel from the Good News Church knocked on the door to "share the joy of advent" with her. Grace had been attending Good News—despite her parents' disapproval—ever since. She knew better than to tell them about the protests now.

On the next drive to Eau Claire, Grace snugged the girl's scarf around her neck. Her empty stomach and chattering teeth made it difficult to keep her verve. She tried to block the wind with her sign.

"Not a . . . choice! It's a . . . child! Not a . . ."

Nearly two hours had passed without an actual woman to yell at, so they had taken to chanting whenever a car drove past. Roger told them it would show people their commitment to the cause. "We might even recruit members this way. You never know!" His eyes looked like dancing flames when he said it, but, as far as Grace could tell, more people were flipping them the bird than giving them thumbs up.

One driver pulled to the curb and put down her window. Her toddlers were in the back seat, mittened hands over their eyes counting as if they were in a mobile hide-and- seek game. The mother chided Grace, "You ought to be ashamed of yourselves. My children don't need to see that!"

A jolt of shame stiffened Grace. Before she could decide whether it was worth upsetting a couple of kids to get their message across, a green Escort pulled into the clinic's lot.

Surprised to see a man get out of the car, Grace stopped chanting. Roger nudged her shoulder and raised his voice. The others followed. "Not a choice! It's a child!" The man slammed his door and headed in their direction. Grace feared he would come across the street. Maybe throw a punch. But he stopped on the opposite corner, his fists in knots, his face a tight red grimace. He yelled something, but the Good Newsers drowned him out. A woman got out of the car, shook her head sadly at the protestors and took the man's hand. They didn't scurry toward the door as the others had but walked slowly, holding hands, their heads erect.

Grace tried to imagine their circumstance, two people who seemed to love each other, plenty old enough to want and raise children. Why would they want to end a pregnancy?

Then, it occurred to her: maybe they *didn't* want to. Maybe they wanted their baby but for some reason couldn't bring it into the world. She'd read about babies whose brain stem never developed, whose lungs were the size of raisins. She wondered if the couple had asked God to take their baby and, if so, why God would answer her prayer and not theirs?

The next week, she told Roger she couldn't go to the protest because her parents wouldn't let her use the car. Besides, she thought she felt a cold coming on. "Don't be silly," he said. He'd swing by on his way to the highway. Plenty of room in his station wagon. He had some good news he wanted to share with the whole group. No pun intended. Ha. Ha.

The heat in Roger's car was going full-blast by the time she slid into the backseat with the other Good Newsers. She loosened the Harlequin scarf and unzipped her jacket.

"Yesterday, I got the latest Operation Rescue newsletter."

Roger put the car in reverse and swung his arm over the back of the seat. Grace breathed in the smell of the scarf. Her stomach felt like it was filled with rocks.

"They can connect us up with other churches in the area. We could have someone on our corner five days a week. That would really put the Good Newsers on the map."

"That's great!"

"Why not?"

He continued, "We might even work up to a Cities of Refuge designation."

Grace tried to figure out where his optimism came from. The number of demonstrators had diminished each week since the beginning of Lent. Today's group was small enough to fit in one car thanks to Emily and Harriet backing out at the last minute. Grace was starting to wish she had stuck with her own excuse not to participate this week, too.

"They're turning up the heat on clinics all across the country. It's risky, but Lent is all about sacrifice." He reminded them of the profound sacrifice Jesus had made so their sins could be forgiven, told them no matter how black their souls had become, forgiveness was theirs for the asking.

"Our sins will be washed away in the blood of Christ, making us all new and pure again." His words reached a crescendo like a Sunday sermon.

Grace could almost hear a chorus of "Amens" and "Hallelujahs" ringing through the car.

As the Good Newsers pulled their signs from the station wagon's tailgate, a police cruiser pulled up to the curb.

Roger greeted the officer, "Mornin', sir. Permit's up to date."

"Don't I know it." He motioned for Roger to step aside so they could talk privately.

"You can say what's on your mind to all of us. We're doing the Lord's work here."

The officer shrugged. "We just got word there's been a shooting at a clinic in Pensacola."

The Good Newsers murmured.

"We were told to suggest you skip today—"

Roger reached his hand in the air to silence the group. "All the more reason for us to stay right where we are." As if he had anticipated this development, Roger continued, "Now we have a martyr." His raised voice sounded like he was speaking to a larger crowd than just the six of them. "We need to let those murderers know we're not afraid to stand up for what's right in the land of the free and the home of the brave." His words gained momentum. "Even if it means risking our lives. Isn't that right?"

Grace had never considered risking her life for anything, not even to cleanse her guilty conscience.

"No, you got it wrong." The officer's face was more serious than before. "Victim was a doctor. Shot *by* a protestor. They don't think he's gonna make it."

Roger let this sink in. Instead of exchanging looks of disbelief or horror, the others looked pleased. Grace could feel their chests puffing up, saw a new light in their eyes.

"Serves him right," someone said.

The officer shook his head in disgust. "Look. We don't want any trouble here. There's no telling what kind of response a thing like this'll get."

Roger was undeterred. "Let us pray."

The officer got back in his car. Grace turned her face to the ground but didn't close her eyes.

Roger said a prayer of thanksgiving for all the babies that would be saved in exchange for the doctor's life. Heads nodded. Grace wondered if the doctor had had any children of his own.

"You work in mysterious ways, dear Lord, but we hear your message: the work we do is straight and true. You call us to shield your sheep from more doctors' murderous hands."

Grace fingered the scarf and thought of all the babies whose lives she'd hoped to save when she agreed to join the demonstrations. As far as she could tell, though, not one of the women who had gone into the clinic had changed her mind because of their chanting. The Good Newsers had managed only to offend people they didn't know and scare little kids. Grace felt every bit as guilty as she had before, not because God had granted her wish and ended her pregnancy but because she knew she would have made the same decision as the women going into the clinic. If it had come to that.

Roger's "Amen" resonated like a church bell. "Grace, would you lead us in a hymn?"

She knew he meant for her to sing "Onward, Christian Soldiers" or "Are You Washed in the Blood?" or something else to rouse God's holy troops to action. Instead, she began with the first hymn that came to her lips, a song she had learned—and loved—when her Grandma Emma took her to the Congregational church without her parents' knowledge when she was a child. "Whatsoever you do," she began, "to the least of my brothers."

She stopped and waited for someone to join in. She looked at Roger, the flames in his eyes momentarily suffering from diminished oxygen. Then he caught himself and sang in his baritone, "That you do unto me." The others joined in as she knew they would. They would never leave Roger and Grace singing by themselves.

To Understand

If you really want to understand what happened, first you need to know that I almost didn't get to have Andrew at all. Not because of fertility problems, mind you, but because Don didn't even want the two we already had. "No more," he'd said when Don, Jr. was born five years earlier, and he meant it. But Don also refused to wear a condom, so there you go. Oops.

I thought he would kill me when I told him I was pregnant again. I even sent Don, Jr. and Eddie to their grandparents' house just in case. Those kids didn't need to see their father murder their mother. I know that sounds melodramatic, but when I kissed them goodbye, I honestly wasn't sure I'd ever see them again.

But I had underestimated Don. He did throw a chair and a couple of punches, but, in the end, he pointed his finger in my face and said, "Not one more complaint about money. Ever." It was a fair trade.

The pregnancy was perfect. With my other two in school, I had gotten darned lonely, but having Andrew inside me, there all the time, needing me for his very life, well, I felt more than happy. I felt powerful. And, believe it or not, Don seemed happier, too. Especially in the second trimester when I got that jolt of energy and tackled the projects on my long list of to-do's. I patched the knees of his hunting pants and stripped and repainted the trim in the bathroom. Dinner was always on the table when he walked through the door, and I stopped serving goulash with macaroni, which I loved and he hated.

To understand what happened, you need to know that after almost not getting Andrew in the first place, I nearly lost him once he was born—eight weeks premature and less than four pounds. While I spent weeks at the hospital willing Andrew to live, Don's mother had to come and take care of the other two. That couldn't have been pleasant. For anyone involved. But sometimes there have to be sacrifices when you're fighting for someone's life.

When the doctors finally let me bring Andrew home from the hospital, I didn't trust he was ready. I was sure I'd screw up and he'd slip away. Don pretty much left us alone and worked extra shifts at the plant. Even though we had pretty good insurance, the hospital bills had piled up, and he used that as an excuse to stay away from the baby he never wanted in the first place.

In those early days, Andrew never slept for more than two hours at a stretch. His little tummy was so small it couldn't hold enough of my milk to tide him over. I kept thinking about the fact that all his growing was supposed to have happened inside my body, and there he was, vulnerable, in the outside world. Even when he could sleep longer stretches at night, I would set my alarm and stand in the doorway of his room listening for his breathing. There is nothing better in this whole world than the rhythm of your child's breath in the dark of night. Sometimes, I would stand there and breathe with him before I reset the alarm and crawled back into bed.

Once the danger of losing Andrew had passed, I worried what Don would do. Turned out he wasn't completely heartless, and there were even times when he would bounce Andrew on his knee. Andrew would start giggling, and I could almost see fondness in Don's face. Yet, they never completely bonded.

When Don would slide into his darkness—that's what I called it, but not to him, of course—his harshest words were always aimed at Andrew. By then, the other two had found ways to be away from home as much as possible, so it was only Andrew and me to choose from. The day I stepped between Don's belt buckle and Andrew, I ended up with a broken nose and realized it was time for us to part ways, Don and me. By then, I had gone back to school and gotten my practical nurse's license and a job at the hospital.

Once I had a few pennies in the bank, I served Don papers and moved the kids into an apartment.

To understand what happened, you need to know that Andrew did go to college but dropped out at the end of his sophomore year. The combination of a bad case of meningitis and skipping classes left him passing only two of four courses that last semester. What was I going to do?

I moved my treadmill out of his old room and told him he could move on home. He got a job and started to chip away at the loans he had taken out. It's amazing how much only two years of college can set you back.

At first, he worked at the convenience store where he gave himself a discount on cases of beer. Though I knew his drinking was a problem, I figured as long as he could get himself up for work every morning, everything would be fine. And everything was. Until Dirk came into the store.

Andrew and Dirk had hung out briefly in high school, until Dirk got busted for an underage drinking party. Andrew nearly lost his spot on the basketball team for breaking the Athletic Code of Conduct. I was stupid enough to believe Andrew when he said he hadn't been drinking. Apparently, the athletic director was, too, because he let Andrew off with a warning. Looking back now, I wish I wouldn't have been so trusting. Maybe I could have helped Andrew sooner if there were real consequences for his behavior.

Anyway, in those days, he'd had the good sense to cut Dirk loose all on his own.

Unfortunately, that sense went right out the window once Dirk dropped by the Stop-n-Go and started supplying him with heroin a year and a half ago.

To understand what happened, you need to know I tried everything. I even called the cops on my own son, told them he'd be down by the Fox River in Waukesha shooting up with Dirk. I had followed him there enough times to know the drill. I figured if he got busted and woke up in a jail cell, that'd scare him straight. Unfortunately, by the time the cops showed up, Dirk was nowhere to be found. Andrew was the one who woke up in a holding cell.

You also need to know how it felt to walk into the county jail to post bail for my baby. The place smelled of vomit and urine. It was like the desperation of those people was a thing and it could seep through your skin and swallow you whole. Andrew's eyes were rimmed in red, his skin gray. His stringy brown hair had a tint of green like they had dredged him off the bottom of Pewaukee Lake. I told myself it was from the fluorescent lights.

I never told Andrew it was me who had ratted him out. I feel bad about that, too, but the arrest did scare him enough to go to NA meetings. He was clean for almost a month.

To understand what happened, you need to know how worried I was about him. How much I hated having to work until 7:00 every evening. Those two hours, when I knew he was off work with nothing to do until I got home, crawled. I would be taking a patient's pulse, and, instead of counting heartbeats as I looked at my watch, I would be imagining the scene: Dirk and Andrew shooting up in Andrew's bedroom, making sure to finish by 6:30, so Dirk could get his money and head out before I got home. Sometimes I just estimated my patient's pulse rate and wrote down a made-up number. Close enough. I know that's bad. But no one died because of it.

On those nights, the time couldn't go fast enough. I would wish for a big emergency to distract me. Okay, that's not entirely true. I wouldn't wish for people to be in a car accident or anything. I just wished—if it was going to happen anyway—for it to happen on my shift, so I could turn my attention to something besides my own worry.

One night, a car pulled up to the ER entrance. A kid was pushed out onto the sidewalk, and the driver pulled away. I tried to get a pulse while a nurse bagged him. When the ER doc arrived, he noticed tracks on the kid's arms and called for a dose of Narcan. We watched as the kid's eyes fluttered and he started breathing again. We all clapped. "There's a reason we call it the Lazarus drug," the doc said. Right there, I decided I needed to get a dose or two for Andrew, just in case.

To understand what happened, you have to know that there is not enough Narcan produced for all the OD's, and that it's illegal for me to possess or administer it outside the hospital. You also have to know that I didn't get my son through being born with underdeveloped lungs, a two-story fall from a pine tree, and the worst case of rheumatic fever our pediatrician had ever seen to let him go down to heroin without a fight. Not on my watch.

The next time an OD came into the ER, I stuck a tongue depressor in the hinge of the medication cabinet, so it wouldn't latch and I could go back later and help myself to a couple doses of Narcan. I want to be clear: no one helped me. I stole them by myself. I can't tell you how much better I felt knowing I could save Andrew if he ever OD'ed. The Narcan gave me a new sense of hope and of power.

To understand what happened, you have to know that I tried to get out of work on time last night. All evening, I had the feeling something wasn't right at home. At the time, I tried to blame it on the full moon and the snowstorm, but, of course, I know it really was mother's intuition. The snow had tapered off, but accident victims were still pouring into the ER. Angie, my reliever, was stuck on the side of I-94 waiting for a tow truck to pull her car out of the ditch. There was no way I would be able to leave work on time, so I tried to convince myself everything would be okay. *Maybe Dirk won't venture out in all this snow. Maybe Andrew will just play video games and drink vodka until he passes out.* That was how bad it had gotten: thinking that passing out drunk was better than getting stoned on heroin. But it was.

To understand what happened, you need to know how much I hated Dirk. And I don't use that word lightly. It was almost as if Dirk and I were in some epic struggle for Andrew's life. I was desperate to keep him alive, desperate to hear his breath when I woke in the night to check on him. Dirk seemed just as desperate to suck that life out of Andrew bit-by-bit. Sometimes, I thought he would wait outside the apartment until I left, so he could call Andrew and have a warm place to get stoned. Andrew was probably one of Dirk's few customers who still had a regular paycheck.

On the night of the storm, I drove home from work as fast as I could without sliding off the road. My shoulders crept towards my ears, and I had to remind myself that getting upset wouldn't get me home any sooner. Before I unlocked the apartment door, I took a deep breath hoping to clear my mind for what I might find on the other side. The muffled sound of a rerun of *Law & Order* made me feel better. *Maybe Andrew fell asleep watching TV.* The clock on the microwave blinked 7:05. So, the power had gone out, and Andrew had gone to bed not bothering to turn off the TV or lights. I flicked off switches, walked down the hall to Andrew's room, and strained to hear his breathing through the door.

Inside I found him face down, a puddle of vomit next to his head. I rolled him over to search for his pulse. Nothing. At first, I went into Code Mode and yelled for assistance, then realized there was no staff to back me up.

Narcan.

I sped to my room and grabbed it from my sock drawer. As I ran back down the hall, I pulled the syringe from its package. Slowly, I told myself, as I inserted the needle into the vial and drew the plunger back. In my training, I had gotten so anxious just practicing to give injections that I often pulled the syringe plunger all the way out spilling liquid on my shoe and having to start over. I couldn't afford to waste this dose of Narcan. Andrew's life depended on it.

I scanned his arm for a good vein and couldn't find one, finally shoved the needle into the freshest looking track mark. Steadily, I pushed the plunger willing each milliliter of the medicine to save his life.

Nothing. I slapped his cheeks, yelled his name. Shook his shoulders, started chest compressions. His eyelids fluttered the slightest bit. Yelled his name again.

One shallow breath. Then another.

I let out a sob and stopped pushing on his chest. Only then did I notice Dirk sitting in the chair in the dark corner.

To understand what happened, you have to know that Dirk was dead. His lips were blue. He still had a tourniquet on his bicep, and a needle dangled from the inside of his forearm. He had soiled himself—I could smell it from where I knelt on the floor—and he was cold to the touch. I didn't kill him. He killed himself.

You might wonder why I didn't try to revive him with the other dose of Narcan, which is a fair question. To be honest, I needed to keep it for Andrew. And, as I said, Dirk was already dead when I found him.

I pulled the comforter from the bed and tucked it around Andrew. As I watched him sleep, it became clearer I had to get Dirk out of there. If Dirk was found in my apartment, I knew I would lose Andrew to the criminal justice system for good. This would be his third strike. Come to think of it, his first and second strikes were because of Dirk, too. Dirk was dead. No sense dragging Andrew and me down with him. That was my thinking.

I grabbed Dirk's feet and pulled him out of the apartment. His head thumping on the stairs made a terrible sound, but I reminded myself he couldn't feel it anyway. The downstairs neighbors were in Florida for the winter, and Jackie, across the hall, works nights. I could make as much noise as I needed to get Dirk out of our lives for good.

The snow was coming down hard again. A layer accumulated on my head and shoulders on the long drag to the dumpster. When I got there, I realized there was no way I'd be able to lift his body over the side, so I pulled him behind it into a shadow. The snow would bury him, and I could come out early in the morning and "find" him. By then, the heroin would be out of Andrew's system. I could tell him Dirk was not in the apartment when I'd gotten home. I'd say maybe Dirk was so stoned he wandered off and froze to death. Or OD'ed. Or both.

To understand, you need to know that when I got back to the apartment, the door was locked, my keys and phone useless on the entryway table. And, though there were plenty of logical explanations for why Andrew didn't hear my screaming and pounding, I knew the real reason, as only a mother can. You need to know I sprinted across the street and rapped on the Wilsons' door for what felt like an eternity before they let me in so I could call 911. By then, of course, it was too late. Andrew had gone back into cardiac arrest, that second dose of Narcan worthless in my sock drawer. The time between dragging Dirk to the dumpster and getting back to my door was all it took for my son to die.

I was powerless to save him.

Demise

Miss Caroline Brill always knew it would be one of her students who would cause her demise. She just never knew which one it would be or how it would play out. Ever since she began her career thirty-five years earlier in 1963, she had found herself in many situations, the outcome of which could, undoubtedly, incur the wrath of an impulsive adolescent with access to firearms or a motor vehicle. She had given F's on final exams, preventing seniors from graduating with their class. She congratulated herself on being one of the few teachers left who refused to look the other way when her students turned in blatantly plagiarized essays. And, lest one of them doubt the sanctity of her deadlines, she docked assignments a full letter grade for each day they were late. If they came in a week past the due date, she would not accept them at all. No exceptions.

If she had had to surmise which student would do her in, she would have presumed it to be the young Jason Rinka. When Officer Phelps of the Sheboygan Police Department had visited the English office asking for a sample of Mr. Rinka's handwriting, she provided it willingly, happily, in fact. The request confirmed what she had known from the first day of school: Mr. Rinka was a bad seed. What she couldn't have imagined was that instead of inserting money or a check into a parking ticket envelope, he had written the police threatening notes and signed them with his own excrement. She found this out only after she had handed his expository essay on the Second Amendment to the policeman.

When Miss Brill later learned that it had been the writing sample she provided that had clinched the case against Mr. Rinka and sent him for a stint in juvenile lock-up, she felt a momentary pang, but then quietly congratulated herself on her contribution to justice and enjoyed her fourth hour class in the absence of the boy.

Six months later, however, she held her breath on his first day back in her classroom. She tried to focus on her lecture about the Puritans but kept glancing toward his side of the room, looking for some sign of animosity, some sign that he blamed her for his incarceration. He slouched in his chair, with neither a notebook nor a textbook nor a writing implement on his desktop. He bit his nails and stared at the floor.

That afternoon, Miss Brill made a thorough check of the exterior of her Oldsmobile 88 before carefully inserting her key into the lock. As she slid safely behind the wheel and turned the key in its ignition, she quietly congratulated herself on spending the extra money on a security system.

After a vigilant two weeks without any grief from Mr. Rinka, she decided that he probably wasn't intelligent enough to deduce from whence a sample of his handwriting had come and she no longer need bother herself about him. Indeed, five years passed, and she neither saw nor heard from him again.

So it was that Miss Brill had relaxed her guard in the fall of 1998, her last school year before retirement. She had accepted the position of yearbook advisor and was supervising the taking of group pictures of the extra-curricular clubs. Young Edward Enders had had the audacity to wear a t-shirt depicting a marijuana leaf. Following a lengthy discussion of freedom of speech, and even of the press—he was on the school newspaper staff—unexpectedly, Mr. Enders agreed to turn the shirt inside-out for the photo. Miss Brill congratulated herself on her ability to bend the will of an arrogant adolescent.

When the proofs came back, however, Miss Brill realized why Mr. Enders had succumbed to her authority so easily: he had found another way to express himself. At the exact moment the shutter had opened, he had lifted his middle finger to the camera. The obscene gesture appeared in every proof the photographer had provided. Miss Brill silently chided herself for allowing her attention to be drawn away long enough for Mr. Enders' insubordination and began mentally composing her letter of complaint to the photographer who should have noticed the finger and taken another shot.

Faced with a deadline and her own dented credibility, Miss Brill encountered a dilemma. She would not put the photograph in the yearbook, and she would not be drawn into another power struggle with Mr. Enders at a retake. No, she would take care of this her own way. She took the proof back to the photographer and demanded he airbrush out Mr. Enders and his obscene gesture, at no charge. Later, when she laid out the page, she added Ed Enders to the list of those "not pictured" below the photograph.

She had done this with satisfaction—nay, arrogance—at the time, yet she deeply regretted it when she distributed yearbooks in homeroom that afternoon in late May.

"Hey, where the hell am I?" The anger in his voice was quite something. "I should be right there in the corner flipping off the camera!" Mr. Enders said it loudly enough for her to hear but not so loudly that she couldn't pretend not to. She looked at her attendance list without seeing it.

Everyone—except Miss Monica Fitzgerald, who never ordered the yearbook and skipped school on the day individual pictures were taken—opened to page 101 to look for the missing obscene gesture.

"Hey, man, I was right next to you. I saw you do it." The sports editor of the *Lake Breeze School Newspaper* shook his head. "That's like tampering with the truth or something."

Any other day of the week, Miss Brill would have cast a knowing glance at the other students and asked innocently, *Why, Mr. Enders, what seems to be the trouble?*

But at that exact moment, she remembered that he had missed a week of school to go deer hunting the previous fall. She remembered he drove a black Ford F-150 with detailing. She remembered those trench-coated boys just last month at Columbine.

"That sucks, man."

The ring of the school bell released some of the tension that had crept into her jaw, but not completely.

Her end-of-day rituals would set things to right, she decided. She removed everything from her desktop and reached for her spray bottle of ammonia water.

"Man, I could kill that bitch!" Mr. Enders' voice cut through the sounds of the books being shoved onto shelves and slamming lockers.

She had sprayed a puddle onto the middle of her desk before she realized what she was doing and reached into her bottom drawer for extra paper towel to sop up the cleaner. There was a time she would have marched right into the hall and challenged Mr. Enders' use of language and threatening manner, but today, she just aligned and realigned the contents of her desktop. She couldn't find a comfortable arrangement for any of it.

Miss Brill debated whether it would be safer to leave school while teachers and students were still milling about or to wait until the halls had cleared. Deciding on the latter, she reorganized her briefcase twice before a voice interrupted her.

"Miss Brill?"

A tiny gasp escaped her throat. How had Miss Fitzgerald managed to get so close to her desk without her noticing?

"Yes, Miss Fitzgerald, what is it?"

"I know this is way overdue and all, but I did finish my paper on *The Metamorphosis*." She pronounced the end of the word, "more-FOE-sis." "I just found it under a binder in my car."

Miss Brill recalled Miss Fitzgerald's tearful insistence that she had written the paper the night before it was due, weeks earlier. She claimed she had written it by hand because her family didn't have a computer and offered to tell Miss Brill what it said to show she wasn't lying.

"I am not accusing you of *lying*, Miss Fitzgerald. I simply cannot evaluate a paper that I cannot *read*."

Miss Fitzgerald had left her classroom with an empty expression and slumped shoulders. Now she stood before her with a look of triumph on her face.

Any other day, Miss Brill would have refused to accept it, citing her policy about late work, and sent Miss Fitzgerald on her way. She would have supported her position by pointing out that allowing work to come in after deadlines rendered them meaningless and rewarded student laziness. She knew Miss Fitzgerald well enough to know that an argument wouldn't follow this refusal. Miss Fitzgerald would quietly accept the zero and move on.

Instead, Miss Brill reached for the paper. "I'd like to have a look at what you think about Gregor Samsa."

Miss Fitzgerald hesitated before relinquishing the essay, which was written on notebook paper with the fringe still attached. Miss Brill extracted a large scissors from her top drawer and sliced the frayed edge into the trashcan. She noted that Miss Fitzgerald had framed the title of the paper in quotation marks—as Miss Brill had admonished her students numerous times *not* to do— and had neglected to underline the title of the literary work—as she had numerous times reminded them *to* do.

She motioned her student to take a seat at a desk

in the front row while she took up her red pen and sat behind her own desk. Out of the corner of her eye, Miss Brill noted the girl checking the clock and jiggling her knee. She probably thought she could just drop off her paper and run. Well, it would be good for her to sit there and see what careful consideration she gave each of her students' papers. Perhaps that would give Miss Fitzgerald respect for deadlines in the future.

The introduction rambled a bit, Miss Brill noted, in its discussion of alienation particularly in the American high school culture. Miss Brill made a note in the margin: *I'm not sure it is "culture" you are talking about here. Do you mean, perhaps, social norms?* However, Miss Fitzgerald must have been paying close attention to the lessons about thesis development, for hers was precise and focused.

If there had been more of the school year left, she would have used Miss Fitzgerald's thesis as a model for the other students. Perhaps next year. Miss Brill's pen stopped on its way to the paper. There would be no *next year*. This would be her last class of seniors. Her eyes found the number on her desk calendar—seventeen school days until retirement. She cleared her throat and wrote, *Excellent thesis, congratulations.*

She looked up to identify the source of the annoying scraping sound that interrupted her thoughts. Miss Fitzgerald was sliding her car key back and forth in the pencil tray, her eyes fixed on the movement. Miss Brill raised her eyebrows and stared at her until their eyes met and the sound stopped. The girl's expression vacillated between defiance and fear.

Miss Brill managed a small smile. "Nice thesis." She turned her eyes back to the paper. "You must have been listening when we talked about thesis statements."

Miss Fitzgerald let out a small sound, unidentifiable as a syllable.

What followed in the essay was wholly off the mark for academic writing. It was self-referential—how many times had she reminded them not to use the first-person when writing academic essays?—and even slipped into second-person here and there. At those points, her red pen asked, *Whom are you addressing here?*

One sentence was hopeless: *I mean, when the world is so random that you can turn into a bug without explanation and people don't even question it, and then start treating you like crap because of it, what are you supposed to do?* Miss Brill stopped making proofreader's marks halfway through the sentence and simply wrote in the margin: *This seems to be what Kafka is asking the reader, doesn't it?*

Miss Fitzgerald's tumbling sentences revealed that she was circling ever closer to a deep understanding of the text, perhaps an even deeper understanding than Miss Brill had been able to manage in her thirty-five years of teaching the story.

Recalling the last time she had averaged grades at progress report time, Miss Brill was quite certain that Miss Fitzgerald needed this English credit in order to graduate, and without a passing grade on this essay, even an A+ on her final exam couldn't save her grade.

"I have a proposition for you, Miss Fitzgerald." She closed the paper and centered it on her desktop. "In your final exam, show me that you have learned how to write without using the first- and second-person points of view, and I will give you full credit on this essay."

Miss Fitzgerald's eyes widened, and she tilted her head as if she feared Miss Brill was teasing her.

"This is not an offer that will be made again." She stood up and pushed in her chair.

"Oh, my gosh."The girl hefted her backpack onto her shoulder. "I can't believe it. Seriously?"

Miss Brill nodded and picked up her briefcase. They walked together toward the door.

"Thanks, Miss Brill. Really. Thanks a lot."

"Yes, I'll see you tomorrow, Miss Fitzgerald."

Miss Brill could never know that these would be her last words and that the student who would render them untrue would be none other than the young Miss Monica Fitzgerald herself. As the teacher locked her classroom door, Miss Fitzgerald was jumping into the old red Maverick she had parked in the fire lane of the teachers' parking lot so she wouldn't be late for her orthodontist appointment after turning in her paper. No one could anticipate that her Diet Coke can would spill on the floor, and, as she leaned over to rescue it, that her foot would hit the accelerator instead of the brake at the exact moment Miss Brill stepped off the curb. But Miss Brill did know, as she caught sight of Miss Fitzgerald's horrified face watching her English teacher fly over the hood of her car, that at least she wasn't going down at the hands of a photo-flipper-offer or a feces-writing delinquent. Miss Brill would be finished off by a girl who knew her Kafka.

You Can't Win If You Don't Enter

Well, I did it. My hands are shaking so much I can hear my charm bracelet jingling and my heart's beating in my ears. Out of the bottom of my eyes, I can see my chest heaving, but really my eyes are focused on the ticket in front of my face. I drag my them back to the black and white Magnavox to make sure I haven't just imagined the whole thing, but the lottery numbers have disappeared from the screen.

They've been replaced by the regular ten o'clock news commercials. American Family Insurance agents smile from inside their forest green leisure suits and plaid sport jackets. "Let us take care of all your insurance needs under one roof," they say. They're followed by a Lasso herbicide commercial, which I watch like a hawk even though I know in my right mind that the MegaMoney numbers won't show up in an ag commercial. But I'm alone and afraid my mind has been playing tricks on me. At least if the young, handsome farmer in his tidy barn starts announcing lottery numbers, then I'll know for sure I have one foot in the funny farm and the other on a banana peel.

But the man with the perfect teeth and clean seed cap doesn't announce my numbers. I have at least fifteen more minutes to wait before Cynthia Smith announces the winning numbers again. I pace back and forth in front of the TV, stopping for a second by the phone. Maybe I should call Ma and Pa to see if they stayed up to find out the numbers. Unfortunately, winning the lottery isn't as important to them as it is to me. They just go to bed at nine o'clock and find out the winning numbers in the paper the next day. Pa says he wants to get a good night's sleep before he wakes up to find out he's a millionaire.

The fates being what they are, my old man really will wake up one day to see his own face on the front page of the *Dodgeville Gazette* smiling out from behind a giant cardboard check made out to himself. That's the kind of luck he has. Not me.

While I wait for Cynthia Smith to announce the winning numbers again, my mind starts to wander something fierce, thinking about what I could do with the money. "Whatcha gonna do now?" I chuckle to myself imitating Len Junior's inflection when I say it.

Well, first off, I'll quit my job at *Piggly Wiggly*. No one-last-shift. Just a quick stop in personnel to pick up my last paycheck, then Sa-yo-narra.

And won't my kids be surprised? Whenever I entered the Sweepstakes—and I have entered them all—they would tease me "Do you have stock in the post office or what? You know they're the only ones who make any money off that stuff."

"You can't win if you don't enter!" I pictured the faces of previous winners, people just like me who opened their front door to find a bunch of balloons, a huge check for a million dollars and a cameraman capturing the moment their lives changed forever.

"Don't worry. I'll share my winnings with you even though you're Doubting Thomases." I'd laugh like it didn't bother me as I organized my shoebox filled with copies of entry forms, lists, and claim stubs. But inside, in my right mind, I knew my chances of winning were slim to none. "You can't win if you don't enter!" I'd say again just because I liked the sound of it. Then I'd lick my stamps and hand the envelope to the mail lady. "Bring me some luck, Josie!"

"You bet, Mrs. Hamilton!" She'd give it a kiss before she slipped it into her pouch. Sweet girl. That was three shoeboxes ago, and some of those forms reach all the way back to 1972.

Over the years, I have been picturing what it will be like when I win. In my daydreams, I happened to be with a lot of people—friends, family, customers, co-work-ers—patting me on the back saying, "Way to go, Pat! Couldn't have happened to a nicer person." Which of course would be a lie, but I'd enjoy hearing it anyway. I was even able to hold my "I told you so" inside for all those who doubted my ship would come in. And, of course, people were shouting, "When're you going to quit *The Pig*? Yesterday!?" since I've made it no secret that will be my first move.

Before I let my thinking about this get the best of me, I let my right mind step in. I have ten minutes left to be me, Pat Hamilton, grocery store clerk, wife and mother. I sit down in my TV chair, the green one whose arms are worn down to the stuffing and covered with hand towels to hide the holes. I'm relieved it's Len's bowling night, so I can have these last few moments as myself. Alone.

When Cynthia, in her beige suit and red blouse comes back on the screen and repeats the MegaMoney numbers, my numbers, 8-23-33-34-41-50, I will be a different person. My life will change into the life I've been waiting for, my *When I Win the Lottery Life* will begin, and I'm the only person in the whole world who knows it.

As I pick at the stuffing, I see my living room through different eyes, through a rich person's eyes. I notice the worn carpet, its goldenrod color way out of date. I've hated that carpet from the minute we moved into Len's parents' house and they moved into the modern retirement village. Even then, I thought it was unfair that my first house was someone else's hand-me-down, with hand-me-down green furniture, while Len's parents, who I still love very much by the way, were the first owners of a furnished, modern condominium. Of course, my right mind told me not to be resentful, but the carpeting, worn almost to the mat now, has always made me feel like Hand-me-down Hannah.

What will be the first thing I buy? Now that is quite a decision to make since the first item will be symbolic. As I am picturing my living room with new carpeting and furniture, Cynthia comes back on the screen and my numbers are there staring me in the face: 8-23-33-34-41-50. She repeats them twice, so now I'm sure.

I have won the lottery, and the jackpot on the screen will be mine. $3.6 million.

The real-life winning turns out to be way different from my daydreams. Quieter, more complicated. I decide not to tell anyone until I'm sure what I want to do. Quitting *The Pig* would be a dead give- away. No, tomorrow morning I'll get up just like normal, put up with my last double-coupon day and lose myself in my plans.

And after that? The question is already repeating itself in my head. I know right away what my friends, my family, even my kids, will tell me to do: divorce Len. And don't think I haven't considered it. In fact, I've considered it so seriously that I had an appointment with a lawyer a while back, last summer.

For three days, Len had been dropping money in taverns all cross Vilas County on another fishing trip with his buddies, his fourth "male bonding weekend" of the summer, and we were starting to feel the crunch when it came time to pay the mortgage. We only had $1.37 to tide us by until I got my paycheck. But Len got it in his head to go up to Avery's parents' cabin on Lost Lake. He always got so excited about his weekends away. I did, too, for that matter. A change of pace from his regular demands. But this time it was really starting to cause a hardship. He flitted off to the Northwoods bouncing checks right and left while I sat at home hoping nothing happened to the car or the house or the kids that would take real money to fix.

A few weeks later, I'd balance the checkbook and see how he'd spent his time, in *Bucky's Tavern, Emma & Leo's Homestyle Restaurant*, and the *Burnt Bridge Saloon*. Not to mention plenty of cash he somehow found to lose in a poker game.

On the day of The Big Fight, I had no intention of letting him out of the house—at least not without a good argument. We got our voices up to a fever pitch before he finally looked at his watch like someone was waiting for him and slammed out the door. I stayed home and fumed the entire weekend, and when he wasn't back by Monday morning, I called in sick and headed to the lawyer.

He finally did come back—on Wednesday morning, I might add. We managed not to talk to each other for another three days. I finally broke down when I saw the Virginia Slims cigarette butt in the car ashtray. This was the straw that broke the camel's back. "Why does Avery's wife go along on these trips and you never take me?" I wondered what excuse he gave his friends for not bringing me along when the other wives were obviously included.

"What makes you think Avery's wife was. . . with us?" Len looked like he had no idea how I could have found out. When I told him about the butt, he looked all amazed like I can't put two and two together. "DeeAnn is the only wife, and she doesn't spend any time with us anyway. Avery brings her along to clean the fish and cook."

I don't believe this for a minute. I know for a fact that cooking isn't DeeAnn's strong suit because she's constantly buying food in the deli section and passing it off as her own. She admitted it. Speaking of admitting, I have to admit I do like the peace and quiet when Len is gone. I just wish he didn't fritter away so much money while he's at it.

For months, I've tried to stay good and mad at Len, so I could follow through on the divorce I got rolling when I visited the lawyer. But Len isn't a monster or anything.

He doesn't beat me. Actually, he's only hit me once or twice in all our married life, and those times I'm sure I did something to egg him on anyway.

But now that the word *divorce* is in my head, it's there to stay until Grandma's old mantle clock chimes midnight. Len'll be home any minute, so I shuffle off to the bedroom without even stopping to brush my teeth. I want to make it look like I'm sound asleep when he gets home. In my state of mind, I'm liable to give something away if I have to talk with him face-to-face. I slide the ticket under the insole of my work shoes and climb into bed.

Almost on cue, I hear a car door slam outside, and the normal Wednesday night routine begins: drop jacket and bowling ball in the hallway, look in a cupboard for something to eat, find nothing, drink water from the jug in the fridge, stop in the bathroom for a pee, take off clothes and leave them in a heap on the floor, let out a huge sigh and loud fart while falling into bed. This is so regular, so normal, I'm tempted to get up and check my shoe to make sure I haven't imagined the whole thing, that my life really is about to change.

I can feel the heat of the divorce papers I have hidden in my underwear drawer.

At the lawyer's office, the originals are waiting for me to get the nerve to go through with it. I told her I wasn't quite sure I'd be able to swing being on my own financially, that I'd let her know when the time was right. Well, no right time presented itself for six whole months. Just when I've gotten nearly fed up with Len's snoring or his tracking mud through the family room or his buying yet another hunting rifle, he'll let up a little. He'll spend more time away from home. Actually remember to fix something around the house that I've asked him to.

I'm sure he doesn't know about the papers in my drawer, but sometimes I'd swear he can sense they're there.

Well, the ticket in my work shoes could take away the biggest reason for staying with Len, but what about the other ones? Even though he hasn't always been the best husband, there's a lot that comes with being divorced. What would Ma and Pa say? Probably, "Hurray!" but you never know. Last I checked, the Catholic Church still frowns on divorce. I can't imagine how embarrassed it would make Len to have to tell people I left him. He does have a temper when he's ashamed.

And then something hits me.

He'll get half of my winnings! His reward for all these crappy years of marriage will be half of my money. Now, I don't deny half of the fault in this marriage, but, honestly, it wouldn't be fair for him to cash in on all my hard sweepstake and lottery work. He's always poo-pooed it, in fact. But in a divorce, this will be his ticket to riches as much as it is mine.

Now, my brain is working overtime. I'm tempted to hop out of bed and start pacing. The idea of setting the bed on fire even pops into my mind, just for a split-second. But that isn't my style.

I don't want to kill him. I just wish he'd up and disappear.

I spend the rest of the night thinking about what I'll do and how I'll do it and about how tired I'll be at *The Pig* in the morning. Soon, the lottery people will narrow down where the ticket was purchased, and it'll become harder and harder to sit on my news. I have to make a plan.

Could I start divorce proceedings before anyone knows about my winning?

Maybe there's some sort of statute of limitations or something like that. But I know I'm fooling myself. Len's been the major breadwinner of the house for years, so he'll be entitled to half the income that he made possible. I'd expect as much from him, but I'm surely not of the mind to just give it to him. The same laws that protect other women from their good-for-nothing, selfish ex-husbands will now "protect" Len from me.

I toy with the idea of disappearing myself after collecting the money, but that's something characters in my romance novels do. I've got my kids to think about. And Ma and Pa. With my luck, they'd declare me dead, and Len would find some way to inherit all my money.

It's not until I've wrapped Len's second sandwich in Saran Wrap in the bright morning light that another thought occurs to me. If I wanted, this could be the last lunch I'll ever make for him, the last thermos of coffee I'll ever pour. Instead of giving me a light, free feeling like I'd expect, this makes me feel like I'm carrying a queen-sized sofa-sleeper up three flights of stairs by myself. I've never lived alone, never not had someone to clean up after. I've always had someone else's clothes to wash and food to fix. And don't get me wrong. More often than not, I think these chores are a royal pain. But, still, it's all I've known my whole life. The thought of being alone is almost worse at this moment than the thought of staying with Len. Almost.

Could I find someone else? How could I ever begin dating again? Again?! I've never really ever dated in the normal way at all. Len was the only date I ever had. Plus, I'd never know if the guy wanted me or my money.

When Len comes down for breakfast, he acts the same as every other day. I get to scrambling his eggs and nearly forget what is making the bottom of my right foot so hot. But I'm reminded of it again while we watch the morning news and the numbers are shown to us not two but three times. Len doesn't even comment.

On the way to *The Pig*, I run into everyone I usually do. They all look the same to me. I wonder if I look the same to them. I hope so since I'm really not ready for anyone to know yet. They'll know soon enough, though. They all will.

I follow my morning routine setting up my cash register, wiping down the conveyor belt, stocking my candy and magazine shelves. As I do every day, I buy my pack of Juicy Fruit to get me through the day and almost laugh out loud when I realized that my first purchase as a rich woman is a pack of gum. But I'm not quite rich yet, I remind myself. No one knows.

And, guess what? A month later, still no one knows. A couple weeks ago, the paper announced that the only winning ticket was purchased at our *Piggly Wiggly*, and everyone has been marveling at the fact that someone has waited so long to claim the money. The stories have been interesting, too. Maybe the winner went on vacation and doesn't know yet. Maybe they died, and no one knows they had the ticket at all. Maybe the ticket got washed in a pair of jeans and was ruined. The other checkers have been combing their brains trying to remember the regulars who bought tickets and whether they bought tickets that day. No one even brought up the possibility of me, and I'm the most regular of all the lottery customers. Sometimes we don't see what's right under our noses, I guess. In fairness, I've been doing a pretty good job of hiding my secret. It's even become kind of a game. I'm clever, too: I've been buying tickets faithfully ever since I won.

Now, you're probably thinking that my right mind is on a long lunch hour, but I know what I'm doing. As soon as the time is right, I'm going to put my plan into action. Just wait and see.

For Your Service

At first, when I roll my wheelchair into *Somewhere Else*, I can't put my finger on what's different. Bert is sitting in his spot like always, a pile of singles and a half-finished drink in front of him. Mike is drying glasses behind the bar. I can hear the crack of pool balls in the backroom. Everything is the same. Only different.

Luther's not in his regular seat.

I push my wheelchair up the ramp to my spot at the bar, and Mike turns over a glass. "Kev, my man, what's up?"

Usually, I'll say something clever like, "My dick for Kelly Clarkson," or "The price of gas," but tonight, I tell the truth. "My heart rate after wheeling my ass up that ramp."

He laughs. "Yeah, well, good thing for you the old man put it in before he sold me the place. Otherwise, I'd be hiking your drinks to you at a table in the back." He pulls on the Miller tap handle and slips the tilted glass under the stream, blots the bottom on a bar towel. Like clockwork: "Bert thanks you for your service." We both let out a grunt that could pass as a chuckle.

Ever since I got out of the VA rehab and started coming here, Bert has bought my first beer, thanking me for my "service." He's one of those guys who yells comments at the TV or tosses his two cents into the group banter, but the only direct interaction I've had with him is my first beer and his mouthing, "Thank you for your service," from down the bar. We raise our glasses to each other and take a nice big swallow. Part of me wants to yell down to him that he shouldn't be thanking me for the "service" I provided on behalf of the U.S. Government, but it's easier just to smile and say thank you.

I'm glad this will be the last beer he will ever buy me. Maybe when I'm gone, some other vet in a chair will take my place. Bert is usually so shit-faced by the time I get here, I doubt he'd notice if some other guy in coffee-stain camo wheeled himself up to my spot.

While I drink my beer, Bert, Mike, and I yell some Jeopardy answers at the TV. "What is retribution?" "What is the Appomattox Court House?" Bert makes it through all the questions about the Civil War. Mike and I take turns getting the ones about movies of the 90's. None of us gets the Final Jeopardy answer: "What is The Reformation?"

I push my empty glass forward to let Mike know I'm ready. The second beer will be on him; then it'll be time for me to pull out my wallet for number three. The guys playing pool in the back put their cues on the rack, down the last of their pitcher and head out. It is long past time for Luther to come in, but the front door stays closed.

Mike slides the beer and some pretzels my way. Usually I'll polish off a bowl or two, but tonight I pass. I'm on a liquid diet.

When I'm halfway through my fourth beer, *Wheel of Fortune* is ending, and I realize I didn't guess even one of the puzzles. Didn't even try. Still no sign of Luther.

Maybe I should be glad he's taking the night off. With his blind eyes that seem to see everything more clearly than I do, he just might say something to make me see my situation from a different angle. He's one of those guys who will sit silently through an entire conversation about whatever Fox News has been covering all day, nursing a beer while the rest of us get so lathered up it feels like we're speaking for the whole human race. The black-and-white of it feels so good. Then Luther will come in with, "You all *might* be right about that." He'll leave a good long pause, so long it would be impossible not to consider the opposite, which is, of course, "You all might be *wrong*." He'll point out something that completely turns the issue upside down. Pretty soon, the suds are getting rinsed down the drain, and the rest of us, even though we haven't changed our minds, all of a sudden aren't quite so vocal about what we were so sure of a few minutes before.

When the Abu Ghraib shit broke, I could see the conversation going that direction. With the jukebox playing in the background, we watched the coverage on CNN. The music was so loud Mike had to read the Closed Captions to Luther so he could keep up. My fellow drinkers described the photos so Luther could picture it in his mind. They all had their opinions and were more than happy to share them. Bert's voice was the loudest. "Hey, man, it's war. You wanna be a terr'rist, you gotta pay the price."

Despite what I knew, I liked the way it sounded. So strong. So sure. It almost took away the rock that still sits in my stomach.

I could see Luther getting ready to tell us we *might* be right.

In about two goddamn minutes, though, I knew they'd be looking to me to speak for the whole fucking military. I also knew that if I started talking about it, there was no way I would be able to stop. Before they got a chance, I headed for the bathroom. Slipped out quietly when I was finished, didn't even go back for the pile of bills sitting next to my half-full beer.

"You ready?" Mike is holding up my empty glass. I look at the door hoping to see it open and let in Luther, so I can feel right again. It stays closed.

I nod. "Hit me again. While you're at it, give me a fifth of vodka, too, will ya?" I throw some more money onto the bar next to the five and singles. Mike doesn't even get the beer to the coaster before I take it from his hand and pour it straight down my gullet, like I'm nineteen again, doing a beer bong down by the lakefront at my going-away party.

I grab the vodka bottle from and push myself back from the bar.

"Don't you want to hang around a little longer? See if Luther comes in?"

"No, man, it's time." It is definitely time. "You can tell

him hi for me." I open the bottle, lift it in a toast to Mike and Bert and take a swig. "And, 'bye'." I cap the bottle and slide it next to my hip in the chair, maneuver to the top of the ramp and let myself go. "Keep the change," I call over my shoulder.

"That's too much, Kev."

I can tell he's stretching across the bar trying to give some back. I brake at the foot of the ramp. "Nope, it's just right. Do something nice for your old lady." I wave backwards. "Adiós!"

A couple I don't know are coming into the bar. For no good reason, I get a flash that the woman could be Ellie. Of course, that's ridiculous. The woman walks past my chair without looking down at me, but the guy steps back holding the door to let me out. Before I can thank him, he is thanking me. Again, for my service.

The night seems extra dark and quiet as I head toward home. Maybe it is always like this, and I just haven't noticed. After a few blocks using my regular route—down the driveway of the *Open Pantry* to get enough momentum to get up the incline at the corner of Edgewood and High, crossing to the opposite side of the block where the roots of the old maple have made the sidewalk squares cockeyed—I decide to make it easy on myself and glide straight down the middle of High Street for the last four blocks. Maybe someone will run me down and save me the trouble of taking myself out. But no one does. All I get are a couple long horn blasts and a "Get the hell out of the way!"

I wheel myself up our driveway and stop at the wooden ramp Mom and Dad tacked onto the front of the house before I came home from rehab. When I see the light in the living room, I realize I'm not ready to go in.

I push myself to the side of the house where I can't be seen from the street, lock my brakes and take another swig from the bottle. When I swallow, it feels like a deep, relaxing sigh. The moon is just peeking over the chimney. That and the taste of vodka remind me of Ellie's first night back from college after her freshman year.

We were trying to act like nothing had changed, but the pretending required a few extra shots and a joint. The more we smoked, the more depressed I got. When *Us and Them* came on the shuffle on her iPod, I told her I wanted them to play it at my funeral.

She took out her earbud and made me repeat myself. I took the other one out of my ear and told her again.

"Make them play it. At my funeral. Promise?"

She turned off the music. "Who the hell talks about their funeral when they're getting high?" She took the joint from me and took a big toke. I hadn't told her about flunking out of tech school or that I had signed on for two years active duty, another six in the Reserves. This would be my last joint for a long time. Maybe forever. I had two months before I had to pass the piss test and start Basic.

She reacted about the way I had expected her to.

"How could you be so stupid?"

It was no secret how Ellie felt about war and the military. But then she had brains and parents who could afford college. I had neither. I turned the recruiter's spiel into words that sounded more like mine to try to convince her it wasn't such a stupid idea.

"Besides, it's not like we're at war or anything. In two years, I can go to school on the G.I. Bill."

"I don't care if you never shoot a bullet, you'll be as guilty as everyone in that damn army."

Suddenly, nothing seemed more important than my funeral song.

"Promise me you'll make sure they play it."

She had a tear in her eye, but I couldn't tell if it was from sadness or anger.

"Fine."

It was my turn with the joint, but she kept the last drag for herself and held the smoke for so long I was surprised she didn't pass out. I wonder if she will keep her promise.

When I let myself in, Mom looks up from her magazine. "You must be hungry. Let me warm up the stroganoff."

I am tempted to let her feed me. It's the one thing she can do for her crippled son. But what I know about people dying is way more than I should, and I'm not about to be found up to my neck in my own shit, thank you very much. No food for me.

I say, "I'm not hungry." To make her feel better, I'm about to tell her I'll have some for lunch tomorrow, but my throat catches when I realize that by lunchtime tomorrow, she won't need to worry about feeding me or washing my clothes. No more scaring the life out of her with my middle-of-the-night screams and thrashing arms. No more wheeling myself into the kitchen the next morning to see her puffy eyes and wonder if I bruised her wrist from grabbing it too hard or if there's a patch on the back of her scalp where I pulled out a handful of hair, while I slept through my own tirade and she tried to comfort my sorry PTSD ass. Never again will she have to be so afraid of me that she takes my dad's rifles to Uncle Jack's house and leaves them there until next hunting season.

"G'night," I manage to say and head to my room.

I listen for Mom settling in bed next to Dad and power on my computer. As I watch the files come up on the screen, I finger the leather pouch I keep to the right of the keyboard. Uncle Vince gave it to me on the day I deployed.

"It's from Nam. Wear it with your dog tags," he said. "Remind you of the tough stock you come from." Vince had come back from the war with endless stories about his heroism, most of which included gruesome details of fellow soldiers' body parts being blown off or his signature punishments for any Viet Cong unfortunate enough to be captured by him.

"Open it."

Inside the pouch was what looked like a brown dried apricot with a small chain running through a hole in the top. I took it out and hung it around my neck hoping it would keep me alive in battle just as it had Vince. "What is it?"

"Ear of the first gook I ever killed."

I felt the burn of bile at the back of my throat. If I really did come from tough stock, I would have taken off that disgusting necklace, picked up my things and walked away—from Vince and from that damned war. Instead, I hid my repulsion and kept the chain around my neck until I could no longer see Vince's salute. When we took off, I bowed my head to remove the ear, put it back in the pouch and slid it to the bottom of my duffle.

I carted that goddamn thing to the other side of the world and back. Turns out the ear did keep me alive in Afghanistan, but now I wish it hadn't. It makes me sick to keep it, but I can't seem to throw it away.

Like the photos.

They appear as thumbnails on the computer screen and make the pictures taken at Abu Ghraib look like patty-cake. When I expand each one to fill the screen, it is as if they were taken in Sense-Surround. I smell vomit, iron, burning pubic hair. I taste leather and boot polish, onions from my MRE and sweat that isn't mine. Electrical currents slice from my testicles to my spine and back again.

Since I downloaded these pictures almost a year ago, I put on my camo and look at them every Sunday night, hoping for the weight of them to lighten, to see them through a lens that keeps me from being a monster even though I was only the guy holding the camera. I never did one thing to those prisoners. That's how I kept myself out of it, in fact. The cataloguer of history doesn't participate. You *might* be right about that.

I wish for the courage to get rid of them, flush the memory card down the toilet, run a magnet over my hard drive. There's no good that can come from them for anyone still living, and those who deserve justice are long dead.

Still, I know people have a right to know what's going on. I heard the President is talking about sending more poor bastards over there. More kids like me to get their legs blown off by IEDs. I wonder if these photos would change any minds.

I also know that these pictures will make a hell of a story for Ellie. The biggest scoop a *Trib* intern ever had. Maybe I can make up for being such an ass at my going-away party. She'll probably see me as a monster at first, but maybe when she calls my mom to tell her about *Us and Them*, she'll also see that I did the right thing in the end.

Ellie's email address is in my contacts list. I open a new email and try to think of what to say. After typing and deleting several paragraphs in which I apologize to her, to my parents, to the poor Afghani bastards, I write a long bit trying to explain how someone like me could stand by and take pictures of my buddies acting worse than animals. By the end of the email, I realize I'll never understand it myself. I hit "Select All" and "Delete." Keep it simple: "God only knows, it's not what we would choose to do." I add, "I'm sorry. You'll never know how sorry."

It would take forever to attach all twenty-seven photographs, so I choose the five worst and begin the upload. While the progress bar marches slowly toward the right, I drop the camera's memory card on the floor and roll over it again and again until it's a collection of blue plastic shards. Mom will vacuum them up without knowing what they are. Once the photos are safely in Ellie's inbox, I'll delete them from my computer. With any luck, Ellie will live up to the reporters' code and not reveal her source.

When I push "Send," a warm sense of peace flows through me. People toss that word around all the time. They get this nostalgic look on their faces, like peace is a return to childhood, innocent and untroubled, but that's nothing compared to how it feels to dissolve the boulder in your gut, knowing that soon you'll get yourself out to Lake Michigan where you'll alternate pills and booze—gradually—so your body can absorb them. Everything will slow down and that mountain of guilt, your monster mask, will disappear, leaving real, pure peace that no child could ever possibly know.

I wheel myself to the bathroom to retrieve the vial of sleep meds I picked up at the VA last week. The nurse seemed relieved I was able to answer all the psych questions in the negative and I was just a case of temporary insomnia. I swallow a few of the pills. Might as well get this thing started. I tuck the vial in the pouch that hangs from the arm of my chair and push myself backward. The chair stops dead. The wheels won't budge. *Fuck, Dad, why leave the bathmat out tonight?* My brain instructs my left foot to unjam it, but, of course, that foot is in smithereens in Afghanistan. Once again, I try to push my wheels forward then back, forward, back. The mat gets lodged deeper and deeper. The more I struggle, the more stuck I get.

When I lean forward to pull out the mat, I lose my balance and land with a thud on the tile. I listen for a sign that my parents heard. But the house is quiet. With all the booze in my system, I'm not feeling solid enough to get back into my chair, so I start to pull myself back to my room with my arms. Without legs to help push, I have a much harder time than when I did this drill in Basic. Halfway to my room, sweat begins to roll down the side of my face. I stink of booze. Should have waited to take those pills. Mom and Dad can't find me—dead or alive—face down in the hall in the morning. I've put them through enough already.

Sound off, one, two. Sound off, three, four.

The voices of my platoon provide a slow, steady cadence. *Mama, mama, can't you see...what the army's done to me?* How long was I in the bathroom? Is there still time to abort the mission? Maybe with our slow Internet connection and my dinosaur computer, all I have to do is get to the machine and unplug it. I'll try again tomorrow. I still have plenty of pills. Maybe enough vodka, too. Tomorrow, I won't cut the timing so close. I'll schedule the email to be sent long after I'm already at the lake and feeling no pain.

Or maybe I'll do what I should have done from the start. Destroy the pictures. Move on. To hell with someone else's stupid-fuck actions. Fuck the poor losers with their crushed nads.

You *might* be right about that.

Brush Strokes

To be naked is to be oneself. To be nude is to be seen naked by
others and yet not recognized for oneself.
Nudity is a form of dress.

–John Berger, *Ways of Seeing*

"Why thank you, Mr. Buttons. I think it's a pretty good likeness, too."

Anna releases a contented sigh as her brush pulls crimson across the canvas. She leans back and rubs the cat under his chin. Her artwork has never come so easily, the images in her mind practically painting themselves. Maybe this is what the others at the Institute meant by "channeling" when they talked about the creative process. At the time, Anna thought they were just a bunch of shallow blowhards who dressed as if they were pieces of artwork themselves.

She tries to push aside the possibility of their having been right, but she can't deny how she feels right now watching her painting come to life. As she stands back to admire the canvas, Mr. Buttons jumps onto the table next to her easel. "Mr. Buttons, no!" He knocks the jar over and starts lapping up the contents.

Before she can grab him and place him on the floor, he leaps off the table, trotting red paw prints across the studio floor.

"Oh, Mr. Buttons." Anna rights the jar, screws on the cap and mops up the mess. Thankfully, the painting is nearly complete. She holds the jar up to the light to see if there will be enough to finish.

"Good thing." She smiles as she swirls around the liquid. "No way Max'll give me any more of this stuff." Anna drops her brushes into the jar of turpentine and turns off the light above the easel. Enough for one day.

Weeks earlier at *Gallery Tamsin*, Anna took her time studying a nude in the back corner. She pretended to be immersed in the painting as the gallery assistant—from the website, she knew his name was Max—finished his conversation with another artist. Their mood was light, the artist thrilled that one of his paintings had finally sold.

"Maybe you're my good luck charm," he said.

Anna could hear the flirtation in the artist's voice and imagined him standing just a little too close to Max.

"See you next week." The sound of a chime signaled his exit.

"You like the edgier stuff, I see."

The closeness of Max's voice startled her. Breathing through her nose, she smiled her crooked smile. "Actually, this is a little tame for my taste."

He lifted his eyebrows and took a step closer. His body flinched, and he reached into his back pocket, flipped open the phone, and read the text. "It's Tamsin." He glanced out the window. "Tornado warning. She wants me to close early."

As if on cue, thunder rolled across the sky. Anna tuned in to her breathing. Two counts in. Two counts out. A warning siren began to clear its throat.

"Tell you what," he looked out the window again, "you don't want to go anywhere until the storm passes."

Anna tried to make her face neutral. She hated it when other people sensed her fear.

He gestured toward some steps. "Why don't I show you some of my stuff? You said you like edgy."

Anna tensed, looked out the front window. The yellow-green tint of the light outside reminded her of the day a tornado had decided to use Barneveld, her hometown, as a piñata, whacking the life out of her parents and little brother, too. "In the basement?"

"Yeah, Tamsin says my stuff is too offensive to put on the main floor. You're not squeamish, are you?" His tongue traced his lower lip.

She forced a laugh. "You've obviously never seen my work."

"I should've known." Max's eyes sparkled.

She kept it to herself that he *had* seen her art six months earlier when she'd emailed him some thumbnails of her paintings in hopes of getting her own show.

She had probably sent them too soon. David had suggested she wait, that she was still too fragile, but she hadn't listened. So when Max's thanks-but-no-thanks reply came back into her email less than thirty minutes later, she'd tucked it neatly in a mental box titled, "Deal with this later."

She had left it there in the dark—no sense in picking old scabs—and had gotten back to work. Little-by-little, she could feel herself shedding the constrictions of the Institute, making bolder strokes, taking bigger risks on the canvas. Her latest paintings were definitely a departure from the fruit and seashell still lifes she had been painting not so long ago. That's what had given her the confidence to visit the gallery in person. If Max didn't like her old paintings, he just might like her new ones.

As she followed him down the steps, she noticed a few grey hairs in his thin, brown ponytail. The smell of basement and oil paint filled her nostrils. At the bottom of the stairs, she caught sight of an easel and supplies in the corner. *How can he paint in this light? It's like a dungeon down here.*

Max pointed to a portrait by her shoulder. "I call that *Bitch Squared*." A disembodied woman's head sported bloody fangs, red eyes and a Medusa-like head of hair. "Inspired by my ex-wife."

She studied it politely and was going to ask about this Medusa but thought better of it. There was no telling how long the "bitch" had been an "ex" or whether painting her portrait had dissipated his hatred of her or fueled it. Fueled it, if she had to guess.

Max ducked back through a doorway to the next room. "You coming?"

The muffled roll of thunder from above urged her forward. She stepped around a half-dozen art crates, paying attention to each step on the uneven floor. She felt a little like she was walking on the deck of a moving tugboat.

He swept his hand in front of a huge painting as if he were revealing a new car on a game show. His expression reminded her of a child showing a crayon self-portrait to his mother. "These are my grandparents. They loved playing cards." The couple wore peasant clothes, Grandma in a headscarf. Light twinkled in her brown eyes. "See that?" He pointed. "The cards are all *Penthouse* covers."

Anna squinted to see the big-breasted, naked women spread-eagle on the back of each playing card. Heat rose in her cheeks. She took a step back and tried to focus her attention away from the cards. Breathed.

"My grandpa was a dirty old man. I couldn't get enough of his *Penthouse* collection. Not that he ever knew I found it, of course." Again, with the tongue.

A faint sense of recognition of one of the pictures nagged at her until she realized where she had seen it before. Anna was not sure if the rumble in her chest came from thunder upstairs or the pounding of her heart. Then she realized: it was the magazine cover her cousin, Yancy, had liked best during Wednesday afternoon "playtime." While Aunt Eileen was volunteering at Hope House, she left Yancy in charge of watching Anna after school.

The afternoons would begin with Yancy concocting a special treat, ice cream with maraschino cherries or chocolate chip cookies topped with Cool Whip. She didn't think it strange, at first, that he had her sit on his lap as she ate her treats. At first she sort of liked the game where he asked her to play the character on the magazines he pulled from beneath his mattress. "See, you can be pretty just like these girls," he said with a kind, soft voice.

When he talked her into taking off her clothes while she moved her body into the weird positions of the naked ladies though, with their knees spread way apart or bent over like a dog, often touching themselves *down there*, she knew that what Yancy was making her do was wrong. Especially when it started to make her feel warm and slippery between her legs. And when he took his own *thing* out and started rubbing it until it squirted like a tube of toothpaste, she had to close her eyes and concentrate hard to keep the vanilla pudding with chocolate sprinkles in her stomach.

Max interrupted her thoughts. "Now you can see why Tamsin doesn't let me show these upstairs."

But that doesn't keep you from bringing people down here to look at them.

He disappeared into the next room. A clap of thunder shook the foundation and made the lights flicker. It occurred to her that the deeper she went into the basement, the longer it would take for someone to find her body if there were foul play. The storm siren seemed to get louder. Just ten more minutes, she told herself. Ten minutes and she could get the hell out of here.

"I saved the best for last. C'mon."

The next room held three floor-to-ceiling panels, each painting of a different *Blue Velvet* movie poster. The first a beautiful brunette, her bare neck exposed, draped over the arm of a man whose face was obscured by shadow. The second was the French version with a man peeping through closed blinds. The third, the bottom half of a woman in garters and black stockings, her ankles bound and blood dripping from the pocket of the pool table to which she was tied. The images had been rendered in Warholesque color schemes: chartreuse, magenta, and turquois.

Max leaned closer. "You know what's really cool about these?"

Anna could smell the cigarettes on his breath. She could tell he wanted her to guess, but the tightness in her throat prevented it. She shrugged instead. Let him dig his own grave.

"They," he paused, flicked off the light, leaving them in deep blackness, "glow." Anna could feel her pupils dilating, grasping for any light that might still remain in the subterranean cave. He flicked another switch bathing the room in black light. Then she saw it. Eyes that had been invisible with the lights on now glowed, staring straight at her, pure fear slicing the darkness. Another crack of thunder made her jump.

"That was a big one!" Max was closer to her than she'd thought. She shifted her weight to avoid accidentally brushing against him.

"How did you get them to glow?" She was not actually interested in the answer, but she wanted to keep him talking. Give her heart a chance to slow down, her thoughts a chance to clear. "Is there some sort of additive to the paint?" She pushed down memories of another basement. Another storm.

She could hear the shit-eating grin in his voice. "Oh, this is a great story."

The anticipation in his pause was palpable. She let it hang there, knowing he was going to tell the story whether she urged him on or not.

He waited seventeen heartbeats before he couldn't keep it in any more.

"Cat piss!"

She tried to hold her breath but a tiny, "Oh," slipped out. What kind of person painted with a cat's body fluid?

"Seriously," he reassured before she got a chance to voice astonishment. "Cat urine," he sanitized his word choice, "glows under black light!"

She let out her breath. "Okay, I'll bite." Her voice sounded like a small girl's. "How did you get the cat, er, urine?" Anna's mind started a mental Google search to find "animal cruelty" on the list of hits when you search "serial killer." She had always treated her own cats like royalty. Even Mr. Tibbs, the matted stuffed cat, who had soothed her nightmares after the tornado. Until Yancy got at him.

Max chuckled. "I squeezed him." He turned on the light.

Anna squinted with its harshness. "Squeezed him?" She pictured Mr. Buttons hanging over Max's art table, saw Mr. Tibbs' shredded body in a pile in the middle of her bed the day she'd tried to refuse to play Yancy's games and threatened to tell on him. The mutilated cat and the ongoing abuse had scared her into silence. A silence that lasted nearly two years.

"Yeah, I'd pull him in in a big old hug and squeeze him until he let it go."

"Squeezed him."

"Yeah." Max's delight was a third party in the room. "To this day, he's the most affectionate cat. He'll climb up on me and not get down until I give him a big squeeze."

"Huh."

"It smelled so bad I had to put six layers of varnish over it." He meant the painting, of course, though Anna wouldn't have been surprised to find a shellacked cat among Max's masterpieces.

"They're very," she reached for a word she'd heard at art shows at the Institute, "powerful."

She concentrated on keeping the bile in her stomach where it belonged and heard only snatches of his explanation of why he loved the movie, *Blue Velvet*, enough to paint his own versions of the movie posters.

She lost track of how long he'd been talking, but he must have gotten a cue from her silence. "But listen to me. I can go on and on about this stuff. I didn't even ask your name. I'm Max." He held out his hand.

It was warm and rough. Her mind scrambled for a name. The only one that came to her was her wacko roommate from the Institute. "Ellen. Ellen Wilkinson."

"Well, Ellen, I'd love to see your work sometime. Do you have a website or something?"

She took a quick mental inventory of her recent work considering which pieces to bring in. "My website's a mess, but I could bring by a portfolio sometime. Are you here every day?"

A muffled all-clear siren called from above. They walked to the foot of the stairs.

"I won't be in again until next Friday. If you come right before closing time again, we won't be interrupted."

The all-clear siren sounded a second time and Anna said, "Perfect."

The painting is coming along beautifully. Anna has draped the subject on a red velvet couch, one arm behind his head, the other running the length of his body, his left hand leading the eye to his small, flaccid penis peeking out from a bush of salt-and-pepper pubic hair. She has angled his torso in an impossible position to reveal as much of his body to the viewer as possible. He has one knee bent, the other straight, and, for anyone who cares to look closely enough, an extra toe on his left foot. Just for fun.

She can't seem to get his belly paunch right—too much like the Pillsbury doughboy—all smooth and pale. With every brush stroke, she hears the annoying giggle from the commercial, as if she is tickling him when she adds shadows to his rolls.

"Shut up!" she yells aloud, startling herself and Mr. Buttons who dashes under the couch.

"Oh, honey, I'm sorry."

She sets down the brush and slides to the floor hoping Mr. Buttons will forgive her outburst. She must sit there longer than usual, but finally, he comes back around and bumps her elbow with his forehead, allows her to rub his chin. *I forgive you*, he says.

From this angle, the painting looks different to her. It lacks something but she can't put her finger on what. Maybe it's the sense of power over the subject that she was hoping to achieve. What did Berger say? The true protagonist of the nude is the spectator himself. Everything in the painting is for his viewing, for his benefit. That's it. Instead of feeling clothed and in power of her subject, she, too, feels exposed.

From the bookshelf, she pulls *The Art of the Nude* and her sketchbook. She tries to picture the color of his eyes and how they looked as he dozed off, but all she can conjure is a flat rendition. Oh well, that will have to do. She practices drawing his gaze directly at the viewer, then a bit off to the left. Traditionally, he should be looking straight at her, but she paints him with his eyes downturned the slightest bit, like he's too ashamed to look her in the eye. She likes that.

Anna didn't wait for David to sit down before she started. "You'd be so proud of me. Ask me why." She loved to tease him, to make him curious so he would probe her for details.

"Okay." He sat. The overstuffed leather chair released a little puff of air. "Why should I be proud of you?"

She slid her feet out of her clogs and tucked them up under her. "Well, you know how you're always telling me I should take a chance with my artwork, get it out there?"

"Wait a minute. I didn't tell you to do that. I said it sounded to me like you were almost ready to get it out there." He took a sip of coffee. "There's a difference, you know."

She hated it when he contradicted her but had to admit he was right. Technically. "Well, anyway, I stopped by an art gallery to see if they'd be interested in showing some of my work."

His eyebrows went up, a small smile visiting his lips. She could tell his fingers itched to write something down, but he stayed still.

"From the look on your face, I'd say it went well?"

"We'll see. It unlocked a painting that's been waiting to be released for a long time." She leaned forward. "I know it's a cliché, but it's like a creative floodgate has opened. I finished three paintings in three days."

The ballpoint pen was in his hand now, clicking like a nervous heartbeat. "Three paintings in three days? That's a lot. You stopped to eat and sleep, didn't you?"

Anna laughed. "Of course. Like I said, they just sort of fell out of me. Aren't you proud of me?"

"What's more important is that you're proud of yourself. That's a big step." Now it was his turn to ask a question. "What inspired you to take that risk?"

"Mr. Buttons."

"Mr. Buttons?"

"Yeah. Cat's talk. People listen." Anna gave him a mischievous grin. "There's nothing crazy about that."

Anna is still unhappy with the painting. The face looks like a death mask, and the reproduction of Max's homage to his card-playing grandparents painted in the upper right corner looks like it was done by a seven year-old. She obscures Max's face enough that he won't be recognizable to those who know him but makes sure he looks appropriately cowed for someone who has been stripped and positioned awkwardly on a couch for all to see.

She stands back and squints. Not enough. Then it hits her: a voyeur. The painting needs a lecherous-looking peeper allowing the viewer not only to objectify the subject but to watch someone else doing this as well. A witness to his shame.

The picture frame on the wall behind the subject becomes an open window, and she begins a self-portrait, taking special care to get her leering gaze just right, a small pink smudge of a tongue peeking out the corner of her mouth.

"What do you think, Mr. Buttons?" she asks but the cat is nowhere to be found. "That's okay. I know what you'll say anyway." Though the painting is fairly abstract and there's little likelihood she'd be recognized in the window, she dips her brush in the black and makes a rectangle over the voyeur's eyes. Just to be sure.

Anna tried to pull into the slanted parking place but was coming from the wrong direction. She did a series of y-turns until she got the Civic pointed the right way. She checked her face in the rearview mirror and popped the trunk. When she came around to find it empty, she made a show of dropping her shoulders in case Max was watching from across the street. For good measure, she walked around to look in the passenger side windows. No portfolio.

As she'd imagined, there were no customers in the gallery at six o'clock on a Friday evening. Max looked up from his computer at the back of the shop and smiled.

"I wasn't sure you'd come back."

He turned off the monitor and joined her at the front of the store. "I was afraid my work might have scared you off."

It was Anna's turn to smile. "Oh, it takes more than that to scare *me* off."

He chuckled. "I set up an easel over by the window, so I can see your stuff in natural light. You said your work is pretty dark, too, right?" He looked at her hands obviously wondering where her portfolio was.

"You're not going to believe this. I left my portfolio at my studio. I feel like an idiot."

Max looked genuinely disappointed. "That's too bad." He raised his eyebrows. "I was looking forward to seeing what twisted stuff lurks in *your* psyche. Should we try again next week?"

"You know, my studio's not far from here." She nodded over her right shoulder toward the door. "Maybe I could run—Or maybe you'd want to come there with me? You could see the real thing, not just photographs. I like to paint big."

Max smiled, his tongue resting limply on his bottom lip. "I don't have a car, but if you don't mind driving me back down here when we're finished?"

She nodded. He flicked off the lights and pushed buttons on the security system. "Let's see what you've got, Ellen Wilkinson."

The old Civic had never felt so small to Anna before. Max's head nearly touched the ceiling, and, with each shift of gears, her elbow brushed his. Instead of repositioning himself to give her more clearance, his body actually seemed to expand.

"Good thing it's a short ride," she changed gears, then pulled her hand back into her lap. Took one turn, then another. "I never noticed how compact this car really is."

"No problem." He leaned closer. "I can see why you don't use it to transport your paintings though."

She exhaled.

"Here we are!"

Actually, they were still a block away, but her announcement had the intended effect of deflecting his attention outside the car while she pulled into a parking space. She headed toward the building knowing he would be right behind her.

"This is the artist I told you about, Mr. Buttons," she cooed dropping her keys in a bowl on the paint-splattered table.

"Hello, Mr. Buttons." Max stroked the cat weaving in and out of his legs. He turned his attention to the windows. "You must get nice constant light in here. Those are north facing, right?"

"Yeah, can't beat it." But the cloudy evening cast the studio in gray.

Anna turned on lamps revealing her artwork. Max stopped in front of the abstract of David carving her brain like a Thanksgiving turkey. He was looking at them in the wrong order. He was supposed to look at *Revelation* first. That's how they were supposed to go. Too late now. It was her turn to play show-n-tell. "I call that *Resurrection*. Can you guess why?"

"Well, resurrection makes me think religion, but I'm not seeing that." He stood back from the painting, squinted his eyes. "I'm getting a violent vibe here for some reason. Maybe it's the point piercing this gray figure here."

"You're good." Anna winked at him. "Sometimes it takes violence to bring something back from the dead, you know? Can I get you a glass of wine?"

"Wine?" Max looked around the studio. His eyes stopped on the glasses on the counter in the far corner.

"Yeah, I don't know about you, but I always find a glass or two loosens me up while I'm working." She walked over to the counter. "I hope red is okay."

"Perfect." Max stepped to the next painting.

Anna poured the glasses making sure to keep the one with the crushed Lorazepam tablets on her right. She handed it to Max as he puzzled over *Retribution*.

"Cheers." Anna held up her glass, so Max could clink it. She took a long, deep drink in hopes he would mirror her. He did.

"That one actually makes more sense if you look at it from the couch." Anna lead Max to sit down and placed the wine on the coffee table.

She sat a cushion away, but Max slid closer. "This is nice." He took another drink of wine. Anna fought the urge to recoil when his hand found her knee. She even forced herself to lean into him slightly.

"Do I see nipples in there, or is that my imagination?" Max's eyes were already starting to look glassy, but his art-interpretation lenses were 20/20.

"Bingo, again!" Anna drained her glass and set it on the floor by her feet.

She watched him drain his glass and offered him a refill. "That's a *Penthouse* cover. Abstract, of course, but now that you know what it is, you probably recognize it. I couldn't believe it when I saw it in your painting the other day!"

Max had a stupid grin on his face and managed only, "Huh," in reply and relaxed into the deep couch.

As his breathing began to slow, Anna told him about the tornado when she was a kid, told him about how, at the first sounding of the emergency siren, she had hidden with Mr. Meow in a cupboard in the basement and how her family searched and called for her and how she'd tried to answer, but no sound would come out until it was too late and they were gone.

She told him about how people blamed her for her family's death when they thought she couldn't hear, speculated that she had some sort of supernatural powers like she was a character in a movie like *The Fire Starter* or *Carrie*. There was even a playground game called, "Ditch the Witch," no explanation unnecessary. Some people blamed her for the existence of the tornado all together.

She told him about how her cat, Mr. Meow, had survived a tornado only to be sent to the pound because Aunt Eileen was deathly allergic and about the stuffed Mr. Tibbs' untimely demise at the hands of Yancy. She told him about Wednesday playtimes. Of how relieved she'd been when Yancy was finally drafted and killed in Viet Nam and how she'd unraveled as the town sang the praises of his perverted ass, hailing him as a hero at his funeral. She told him about how they'd locked her up in the Institute for what seemed like a lifetime until she figured out how to play their game better than they did and they had to let her out.

She told him how disappointed she was that she'd never gotten a chance to make Yancy realize how he'd wrecked her, that she'd never gotten a chance to make him pay.

"But don't feel sorry for me," she laughed into the silent room. "There are plenty of other men in the world who love nothing better than to degrade women."

Anna made sure to tell him that she honestly hadn't gone to the gallery that day to make him a victim. She had sincerely believed her work with David had almost completely silenced her darkness. Honestly, she told Max, she had gone to the gallery only to feel him out, to see if he might give her work another look. Maybe it would be harder for him to blow her off in person than it had been to do it in an email.

And what had pushed her over the edge? She really couldn't put her finger it. Whether it was the *Penthouse* covers, *Bitch Squared* or the mutilated cat. Was it the tornado sirens? She would probably never know.

Anna is careful not to bump the wrapped painting as she pulls it from the back seat. From here, she can see Tamsin gesturing toward the nude, which has been moved from the back of the gallery, and if Anna had to guess, is about to be sold. Tamsin's customer smiles and strokes his goateed chin. He nods and nods. Maybe Anna should get in there and introduce herself to him. "If you like nudes," she might say. But that's Tamsin's job. Probably best not to cross that line, at least not until she gets herself hired to take Max's hours. Tamsin must be getting sick of working on Fridays by now.

Anna catches Tamsin's eye through the window and waves. She crosses the street and, as she pulls open the door, glances at the frayed poster taped to the glass. Max's face looks back at her and asks, "Have you seen me?"

Dry Spell

Rodney Quick was on a mission. Not your usual mission that would require learning how to say "God" and "Savior" in some African language or a slew of vaccinations or a good supply of hand sanitizer. Rodney didn't need to learn anything about the souls he'd been called to save. He knew enough about them already.

This mission Rodney could carry out in English, in his own backyard, just outside of Edgerton on the acres of tapped-out tobacco land abandoned by the tenant farmers who had been paying the property taxes on it since his parents died.

With the ink still wet on his severance check from the GM plant, Rodney pulled down the decrepit *For Lease* sign and stood, hands on hips, considering those fields.

Grateful that summer temperatures had held on, he squinted at the mid-day sun. It would be an hour or two before Tom got off work, so Rodney had plenty of time to kill. He pulled a six-by-six from the pile of lumber in the bed of his truck, screwed on a good- sized piece of plywood, and grabbed the paint. Ever since he was a kid, he never planned his writing right, so the sign ended up cockeyed, but Rodney still felt satisfied an hour later when he stood up and took it in:

"PAiNTBaLL FOR JESUS"
FUN, FOR The GLORY O
f
G
O
D

It needed something in the lower left corner, so he added a crucifix with three beams of light emanating from each side.

As he closed the paint can, the sound of boots on gravel interrupted his thoughts.

Tom and Rodney stood over the sign like they were looking into an empty grave. "Paintball?" Tom held out a crumpled pack of cigarettes, but Rodney brushed it off. "That what you wanted to show me?" Rodney nodded.

Tom lit up and took a long drag. As Rodney watched the smoke leave his nostrils, he was tempted to say, *Ah, what the hell?* and ask for a cigarette. But the pack had already disappeared into his friend's shirt pocket. Tom was walking around the sign like he wanted to take it in from all angles. He stopped and looked at Rodney sideways. "For the glory of God?"

"Think about it." Rodney stuck a toothpick between his teeth. He poured coffee from a dented thermos into its plastic top. "What'd we do when we told our ma's we were going to 5:15 mass on Saturdays?" He didn't wait for an answer. "We went out to Gibbs Lake and smoked and drank and got girls knocked up." He swallowed the last word. "Well, that asshole, Burkhalter, did anyway."

The thought of it pissed Rodney off all over again. He could still see their childhood friend Jenny's tear-streaked face when she'd told them she was in trouble and could they drive her up to Madison to get rid of it?

His tongue shifted the toothpick to the other side of his mouth. "But kids today's doing worse than that. Watched the news lately? Stealing from *their* ma's to support crack addictions. Those kids *need* the Lord, Jim Dean says."

Tom let the air out of his lungs. "Jim Dean, huh?" He reached into his back pocket and pulled out a flask, uncapped it and offered it to Rodney.

Even though he knew Tom was following the code— you always offer the first swig to the other guy—Rodney had to push away the feeling that Tom was trying to throw a monkey wrench into his sobriety. "No, thanks." Once Rodney turned it down, the offer would not be made again. Today, anyway. Like the cigarettes.

Rodney unfolded the paper placemat with his diagram on it and smoothed it out on the open tailgate of his pickup. He turned it so the house was in the upper right hand corner. "Folks can park down here. The battlefield will be here."

Tom squinted at the drawing. "What are these squares and sideways x's all over the"—he looked up at Rodney—"battlefield?" He gazed across the land like he was picturing Rodney's plan come to life.

"Modified deer stands, I'm thinking. For cover." Rodney had saved the best idea for last. "And crosses, of course. Each cross'll have a Bible verse on it. That idea came to me last night before I fell asleep."

Tom polished off the flask and took a long drag on his cigarette.

Rodney's muscles ached. Blisters rose on his palms. September had decided to act more like summer, and the sunburn on the back of his neck felt like someone had taken a blowtorch to it. In his kitchen, he poured himself another cup of coffee and cracked an ice cube out of the aluminum tray. At first the cube stuck to his skin, but once it melted a little, it glided across the back of his neck, sending a frigid trickle down his spine.

The peeling wooden chair grumbled as he sat down to look at the Bible, opened to Deuteronomy. Rodney flipped through the pages of the stiff book. As he tried again to decipher the words, he figured he probably had some kind of reading disability. The way the sentences were written, it was like God had tossed the words into a Yahtzee cup and given them a good shake. This couldn't possibly be right: No one whose testicles are crushed or whose penis is cut off shall be admitted into the assembly of the Lord? He couldn't write that on a cross.

A week earlier over coffee, his AA sponsor, Jim Dean from over in Milton, told him the Bible had wisdom for every occasion. "You just gotta read between the lines," he said.

Unlike Rodney's pristine book, Jim Dean's Bible was a sight. Worn leather cover, faded gold-rimmed pages. The satin built-in bookmark obviously wasn't enough for Jim because there were at least thirty sticky notes popping out the sides and top of the book. When someone brought up a specific failing in a meeting, Jim was constantly snapping open his Bible. He'd run his finger down the page, read over a line, nod his head like now he knew something everyone else didn't. Once in awhile, he'd read the lines aloud, but mostly he kept their wisdom for himself.

Just watching Jim's confidence when he consulted the Bible made Rodney wonder what was in there. When Jim did this, it made Rodney want a drink so bad his mouth watered. He hated this feeling of being on the outside looking in. But Jim looked so damn sure—smug even—as he read his Bible passages, that Rodney couldn't help wanting into Jim's little club with the Lord. He decided right then and there he would come up with something to show Jim Dean he was worthy of membership.

He's gone home and straightaway found his confirmation Bible, surer than sure the first passage he read would hold some insight for him just like Jim Dean's Bible always seemed to. Rodney closed his eyes, opened the book and stabbed his blind finger at the page. *In cases of defiling skin diseases, be very careful to do exactly as the Levitical priests instruct you.* The skin diseases part made him think of Mother Theresa, but Rodney couldn't imagine working with lepers. He heard Jim Dean's voice, "God's love is there for all who seek it."

The next passage he picked at random had something to do with preparing bodies for burial. Ready to give up, Rodney closed the book and rested it on its spine. He let go of both sides at the same time, so it fell open. *Arm men from among you for the war, that they may execute the*

Lord's vengeance. There. It spoke with such clarity, he'd have had to be deaf and blind to miss it.

Now to find some inspirational Bible verses to display on the crucifixes planted in the Battlefield.

"Where're you gonna get the weapons?" It was Day Three of construction when Tom interrupted Rodney's rhythm as he assembled the tallest cross of all.

Rodney put down his screwdriver, pulled a bandanna from his back pocket and wiped the sweat from his face and neck. He pushed down a gnawing feeling in his gut. "Huh?"

"Weapons. You know, paintball guns?"

Rodney resisted the urge to snap, *Now?! Now, you think of this? Where were you three days ago?* Instead, he said, "Don't people bring their own weapons? Like we do at the gun club?" He took off his cap and ran his fingers through his thinning hair.

Tom shrugged. "They'll probably want eye protection, too."

Before Rodney could decide what to do with this new information, Fran Michaels from next door pulled into the foot of the driveway and rolled down her window. "I told Larry you weren't building a fence." Fran always started conversations in the middle. "I told him only a drunk would put in a fence that off-kilter." Tom laughed out loud. Fran's face registered embarrassment. "Oh, no, I didn't mean it like that. It's just I—I heard you were back on the wagon, Rodney." He nodded. She smiled. "Good for you."

"Nice save," Tom chuckled.

"I only meant you must be doing something else over here. Are those," she pushed her eyebrows together, "crosses?"

Glad he had leaned the sign on a sapling facing away from the road, Rodney took a couple steps closer to the car. "Yup. Crosses they are." He knew she wouldn't go away until she was satisfied, so he threw her a bone. "A little project for the youth of the community. I'll invite you over when we unveil it." He curved the conversation away from his mission. "Until then, Larry's welcome to keep hunting the back woods. Seen lots of rabbits around there lately." He waved over his shoulder. "Bye, now."

A coffee-stained mug and a phone book opened to the yellow pages sat next to Rodney's Bible and spiral notebook. He circled the number of Burkhalter's Big Fish Construction in red and absently lit another cigarette.

He practiced his nonchalant voice, propping the receiver between his shoulder and ear while his free hand held down the button. "Frank, it's me, Rodney Quick, long time no see." He took a deep drag to calm his nerves. It would be awkward calling his former high school buddy to ask him for money, but Frank owed him, owed him big as far as Rodney was concerned, and he'd saved the IOU all these years waiting until the moment he needed to cash it in.

Now was the time.

The phone rang. Rodney jumped releasing the button. Instead of his usual, "Yeah?" he blurted out the second part of the script he'd prepared for Les, "I think you and me have something in common."

"What the—?" It was Tom. "Rodney? That you?"

"Oh, yeah, sorry. Thought you were somebody else." Rodney pushed the rest of his lines from his mind: *You and me have found the Lord. I'm starting a business. Thought you'd wanna be in on the ground floor. The crosses are all set…*

"I'm down here at Pete's and got wind of an inspector coming by your property.

You pulled a permit, didn't you?"

Permit? "Aw, shit." It hadn't occurred to him that he'd need a permit to turn agricultural property into a paintball range. What else hadn't he thought of? Insurance. Advertising. A cash register. Why could all this come into his mind when his back was up against the wall but didn't bother to show up when the idea was first grabbing ahold of him?

He could already feel his plan faltering. What had ever made him think he could save a bunch of other souls when he couldn't think his own way out of a brown paper bag? Rodney felt the pull of a beer at *The Union Tavern*. He could forget the whole thing, start drinking right now—skip the embarrassment and kicking himself and go straight to accepting it. Once a drunk, always a drunk.

"Ah…" Tom paused. Rodney knew him well enough to know that Tom's first reaction would normally be to say, *Ah, fuck him if he can't take a joke. I'm taking the afternoon off. See you at The Union. First round's on me.* Instead, he said, "The fat lady ain't sung yet. I'll tell him our permit got held up. Get him to come around in a month or two. That'll give us plenty of time."

Rodney wasn't sure when Tom had gone from saying "you" to "us" about the paintball range, but he liked it. Maybe it was time to get some more people in on the plan.

Rodney broke the rhythm of the speakers before him. "Hi. My name is Rodney, and it's been six weeks since my last drink." He'd skipped the part where he was supposed to admit he was an alcoholic. The other members of the meeting shifted in their seats. Some said, "Hi, Rodney." Others clapped for his weeks of sobriety.

Rodney could tell by their exchanged glances that they didn't believe him about his last drink. "No, really, the reason I haven't been to a meeting lately is because I've been starting up a business venture."

What better group to get in on the action? A room full of people who believed in God and could have used a wholesome activity like Paintball for Jesus when *they* were teenagers.

As if he was imbued with the Holy Spirit itself, Rodney described his beautiful plan for saving souls, preventing drug use and alcoholism, and replacing the income he'd lost when the tobacco farmers jumped ship and he lost his job at the plant. He spelled out his vision, a vision that had never been so clear to him before. He could see the walls of weapons for rent, the boxes of ammo for sale, the permit framed and hanging on the wall of the winterized shed, Tom and him working side by side. "And I'm sure," he started to wrap up, "you all will want to get in on the ground floor."

Where he expected to see smiles and nods and people reaching for their checkbooks, he saw uncomfortable looks and lip biting. He heard chairs creaking as people shifted their weight. Jim stood up. "Ah, Rodney," he applied just enough pressure to Rodney's elbow to let him know his time with the floor was done. "I'm sure I speak for everyone when I say, it's great that you want to do something to honor the glory of God and promote sobriety in young people—" He started to walk back to the chairs with Rodney's elbow firmly in his grasp.

The heat of shame rose in Rodney's cheeks.

"But we have an agreement here not to use meetings for promoting our businesses." He invited the others' support.

Doug spoke up from his perch by the coffee urn. "He's right, Rodney. You don't see me pitching my print shop, now do you?"

Rodney resisted the urge to point out that, by mentioning his print shop, Doug could be considered guilty of self-promotion, too. But he didn't have the heart.

The men started to stand up, and the women leaned over to pick up their purses, searched for car keys. Jim tried to bring the meeting back around. "Why don't I lead us in the Serenity Prayer?" Purses settled into laps. Eyes closed. "God grant me…"

Grateful to close his eyes, Rodney tried to focus on the words swirling around him.

Rodney pulled his pickup onto the gravel driveway. The sun setting over the Michaels' barn gave him that feeling he got nearly every day as six o'clock rolled around. The day was almost done, and the reward for doing the repetitive, mindless work he'd had to do at the plant could start to fade into a shot and a cold one. That feeling

KIM SUHR

like every cell in your body is doing one giant exhale and that question of "What the hell am I wasting my life here for?" fizzles away like the head on your beer. By the bottom of the glass, you're goddamn glad you have the job, to give you that couple extra bucks for a few at the end of the day. You order another one, and it slides down your throat like a dip in Willie's Pond.

Down the bar from you, Henderson finishes his pitcher and wanders over to the jukebox. You know he's going to pick A7, "Ruby, Don't Take Your Love to Town," which signals it's time to get in your pickup and top off your buzz over at *The Union* with your old friend, Tom, who's just getting off work. Walter, the bartender, gives a casual salute. "Thanks for comin' by, Rodney." Like you're an old friend he hasn't seen in years and he can't wait for you to stop back again, even though he knows you'll be back around tomorrow sure as the clock on the wall. You feel bad about leaving him with Henderson's sad eyes, but you know if you stay, it won't be long before you're heading over to the jukebox yourself pushing C21 and singing, "I'm so lonesome I could cry," at the top of your lungs and making a pussy fool of yourself. Yeah, a few beers over at *The Union* would make everything feel right again, but a fresh pot of coffee would have to do.

Next day, Rodney dragged the last of the leftover wood from the crucifixes to the bed of his truck, not caring if they got dinged up by the tailgate. He tossed his tool-box on top of them knowing its latch wouldn't hold. He didn't care about that either. The sooner he put this behind him, the better.

He caught sight of a pile of beer cans at the foot of the *Thou Shalt Not Murder* cross and found an equal number of cigarette butts strewn around the area. At first, he thought they were Tom's, but Tom didn't drink Schlitz or smoke Winstons. The litter reminded him of how many cans and butts they'd left on the shore of Gibbs Lake when they were in high school.

As he bent to pick them up, he heard his friend's truck pull up the drive. Tom parked and sat inside long enough for a stiff pull on his flask. It had been over a week since he'd drunk in front of Rodney, almost like he was protecting him from the stuff. Rodney was tempted to jog down the driveway and join him, but he stayed put. Tom disappeared behind the pickup.

A minute later he strode from behind the truck, something slung from each shoulder. "Hey," he called ahead, "got a surprise for ya!"

Rodney squinted trying to figure out what it was. He took a long drag on his cigarette and flicked it aside. "A surprise, huh? I hope it's a good one."

"I think you'll like it." He held out a rifle with some sort of black plastic container on top of the barrel and what looked like a can of propane hooked on underneath. "Here ya go. Locked and loaded."

Rodney looked at the gun like he'd never seen a weapon before and realized how stupid his plan had been. Here he'd wanted to open a paintball range but had never even held one of the guns in his hands, never pulled a trigger. "Where'd ya get that?" He took it from Tom and propped the stock on the front of his shoulder, closed one eye and took aim at a cross twenty-five yards away. The gun was light, like his pop's old .22, the one he'd used to hunt rabbits.

"Go ahead. Slide the cock back. On the side there." Rodney found the lever and pulled until he heard a click. "Let her rip."

He aimed at the *Honor Thy Father and Thy Mother* cross and squeezed the trigger. The orange splatter on the wood was small but unmistakable. "Damn!" Rodney's voice was so light he almost didn't recognize it. "I still got it!"

Tom tossed him a padded vest and safety glasses. "Let's play." Rodney felt the heat of competition rise in his cheeks.

"I'll start at *Coveting Your Neighbor's Wife*. You start here."

Rodney tucked himself behind *An Eye for an Eye* and watched Tom's long strides toward the tallest cross on the property.

"On my count!" Tom's voice sounded far away. "Ten, nine, eight…"

Rodney could feel his heart beating faster, as it always did in any kind of dangerous situation: ratatatatata. He felt the swelling in his chest of *eat or be eaten*, the thrill of diving from the rocks at Devil's Lake, the rush of joy riding at ninety miles an hour with a bellyful of Mickey's Big Mouth beers. His senses heightened, he could make out individual needles on one of the scrubby pines he'd planted, each one shivering in the October wind. Even his sense of smell was sharper: the aroma of sandy soil, the pine wood of the crucifixes, the traces of the fat permanent markers they had used to letter the posts.

And the smell of fear. His own fear. Like the rancid smell of B.O., it clung to him.

His mouth watered wishing for a quick swig of whiskey before the shooting started.

"One!" He heard the report of Tom's gun. Pop. Pop. Pop. Tom had never been as good a shot as Rodney, and today he was no better.

Rodney crouched scanning the horizon for his competition. Funny, when he'd talked about his idea of using crosses as obstacles, Tom said he was crazy. But with so many of them at different heights and distances, it was like an optical illusion. Rodney saw Tom's camo dash forward to another cross that he would have sworn was twenty yards back. Rodney decided to go full bore to *Honor the Sabbath Day*, shooting all the way. He cocked, shot, and re-cocked the gun and wished Tom had bought an automatic. At this rate, he'd have a cramp in his hand before he got close enough to have a prayer of actually hitting anything.

He made a break for *Jesus Wept* but had to slow down halfway there. When had he gotten so damned out of shape? He heard the thwack of a paintball hitting a cross head high and felt droplets of paint on his cheek. That would smart if Tom ever did hit him. Rodney cocked his gun again making sure to aim for Tom's body instead of his head. He hit the cross dead center.

Suddenly, Tom's shooting stopped. Rodney saw him look over his shoulder, like he heard someone coming up behind him, then make a mad sprint in the other direction. But before he knew it, Tom was down.

Rodney stopped shooting and looked at the end of his gun, as if it had somehow laid out his only friend.

Two hundred yards off, Rodney saw the silhouette of a man with his own rifle barrel pointed at the ground, walking toward Tom. In that second, Rodney knew what had happened. "No!" He broke into a run.

"Stop right there!" The man lifted his gun to his shoulder like he was about to take aim at Rodney.

Rodney dropped his paintball gun and threw his hands in the air. "Don't shoot!" But the lump of Tom at the foot of the cross made Rodney wonder if he really meant it. Would he really want to live if Tom wasn't around? He put his hands down. "Fuck it." Let the guy shoot.

He sprinted to Tom's body, blood pounding in his ears. Rodney whispered, "No, no, no," with each step he took. "No! No! No!" like a machine gun.

He stopped. Tom wasn't a lump at all but was flat on his back, like a shadow of one of the crosses that stood above him. "Tom? Buddy?" Rodney dropped to his knees. He placed Tom's head in his lap. "Tommy. Don't leave me, man. Don't." Rodney blinked his eyes to clear the blurriness in his eyes. He searched Tom's body for a wound he could cover, first his chest, then his belly. If it was a head wound, there should be blood all over Rodney's lap. "Where—?"

He heard a faint groan. Tom's eyelids fluttered. Sure it was his imagination, Rodney kept on begging. "You can't leave me now, Tommy. We've come too far. Tommy?"

Another groan and Tom slowly opened his eyes. Rodney could tell his friend couldn't focus on his face, so he kept talking. "I'm here, buddy. I'm with ya. Where were you shot? Where's it hurt?" Rodney rubbed his sleeve across his eyes and scanned Tom's body again.

"Head," Tom croaked.

"What's that? Your head?"

"I didn't shoot him for Christ's sakes." It took Rodney a second to place the voice behind him. In the jumble of the moment, it could have been God for all he knew. He turned to find Larry Michaels, a dead rabbit in one hand, a .22 caliber in the other.

Rodney was too relieved to be embarrassed or angry. "That right, Tommy?" Now he could see the knot on Tom's forehead rising like a potato.

"Huh?" Tom tried to sit up with a groan.

"Just be still, Tommy." Rodney used a soothing voice. "One of the crosses clothes-lined you. You're okay, buddy." And, as if he was so delighted to hear the words, he said them again, this time with more conviction. "You're okay."

"I come out of the woods and saw two guys shooting at each other. Thought it might be those kids who's out here the other night." Larry set the safety on his gun, laid it next to his rabbit on the ground. He moved to help Rodney stand Tom up. "What the hell is going on over here?"

"That's a goddamn good question." Rodney wrapped his friend's arm around his shoulder and started to help him back to his truck.

When he got Tom settled in the passenger seat of his pickup, Rodney's eye caught the placemat plan that had fallen on the floor. It had a dusty boot print on it and looked completely different than it had just a month earlier. He realized that, instead of being an alternative to drinking, kids would use a night at their paintball range as an excuse to get lit up and play warrior. That's exactly what he and Tommy would have done.

He looked across the field at his plan in life-size. The range was just a bunch of cockeyed crosses with misspelled Bible verses that continued on the next cross because he'd run out of room. Just another example of one of his projects—wild hairs up his ass, Tom called them—that he'd start when he first went back on the wagon. Every time, every damn time, they'd fall apart. And who was there to pick up the pieces when the thing fell through? Tom. Tom was the guy to say, *That's okay, Rodney. Fuck 'em if they can't take a joke*. Rodney put the pickup in reverse and headed toward *Walter's*.

When Rodney came off a dry spell it was always Tom who bought the first round. This time, they'd been gone from the bar longer than usual, and someone else, some guy named Dale from the plant, had made himself at home on Rodney's barstool. At first, Rodney thought about letting Dale know that this was his spot and would he mind shifting down one? Then he decided a lost spot was the price to pay for getting on the wagon in the first place. Maybe he'd learn.

"Let's sit on the corner." Rodney headed for the other end of the bar. "See the TV better anyway." They settled onto the vinyl seats.

"Will ya look what the cat dragged in," Walter tossed a cardboard Schlitz coaster on the bar in front of each of them. This was the time when Tom was supposed to say, "Let me buy this bastard a drink!" with celebration written all over his face. "And one for me, too."

And Rodney was supposed to say, "Don't mind if I do," and order a boilermaker.

Then Tom would say, "Welcome back, old friend." And the two of them would lift up their shot glasses of whiskey, knock 'em back, let out a simultaneous "ah," and take a swig from the beer that came with the shot. After the bartender filled their glasses a second time, Rodney would notice Tommy's face in the mirror behind the bar, with that look like when you've been waiting all day by the window for someone to come home and you hear the back door open and there they are.

Instead, Tom slouched over the bar, his seed cap covering up the goose egg on his forehead. He pretended like he was interested in the game even though Rodney knew he didn't like baseball, hated it in fact. Walter and Rodney looked expectantly at Tom waiting for him to remember his lines. When it became obvious Tom wasn't going to take his eyes from that TV no matter what, Rodney pulled out his wallet and threw a twenty on the bar. "The usual."

Tom held up his shot glass in a brief cheers to no one and downed it before Rodney could pick his up. Their "ah's" missed their cues, too. And the sensation that always felt like home with his first beer after a dry spell didn't bother to come by.

How We Got Our Baby

I had just hefted the last box onto the porch when I noticed a woman striding up the driveway. She wore a hot pink warm-up suit, her hair a brown-red color nobody has naturally. She carried a plate of something covered with plastic.

"Hey, Mags," I called through the screen door, "neighbor's here."

Maggie stopped at the doorway and fluffed her bangs. Her tired eyes had a new light. "Let's meet her halfway."

"Welcome to the subdivision. I hope you like popovers!" The woman straightened out her arms before we were close enough for Maggie to take the plate. From where I stood, the two looked like they were about to embrace, which would have been just fine with me. All Maggie had been able to talk about on the hour-long drive from the city was how worried she was that she wouldn't make any friends in the new neighborhood.

Maggie's "You're so kind" overlapped with the woman's announcement of her name—something like Kristen or Kirsten.

"We're the Beckers." I held out my hand and intro-duced Maggie, then myself.

"We're so glad the place finally sold. You must have gotten it for a song." Kristen gestured toward the realty sign with a *Sold!* tag on top. "It was on the market for such a long time." She paused. "So sad about the Millers."

Maggie's face dropped. We knew the house had been in foreclosure. That's the only way we could ever afford it. But until now, the previous owners of the house were just "that poor family" in our evening prayers. Now they had a name.

"It was so rude of me to bring them up." Kristen brushed the name out of the air with her hand. "What I mean to say is, 'Welcome to Delafield. We're so glad *you're* here.' Where did you move from?"

Maggie told her about our bungalow in West Allis, the car break-ins, the endless stream of visitors next door, the neighbor's pit bull.

"The police would drive through the neighborhood every so often but never found any proof he was dealing drugs." Maggie said. "It was just time to go. Especially because we wanted to start a family." She laid her hand on her stomach.

I squelched the voice that whispered, *You just jinxed it.*

Kristen cooed, "That's wonderful. When are you due?" I could see her planning the neighborhood baby shower already.

Maggie fluffed her bangs again. "I'm not pregnant yet, but now we can start trying."

That wasn't the whole truth. We'd been "trying" for a month, since we made the initial offer on the house.

"Well, that's exciting. It's been so long since we've had little ones in the neighborhood."

"So long? With all the play sets in the backyards, we figured—"

"Oh, those. Most of them are leftovers from when our kids were young. We're all hoping for grandkids to use them some day."

Maggie gave Kristen a friendly once-over. "You look way too young for grandkids."

Kristen laughed. "Tell that to my husband."

Maggie was right. Although there was something about Kristen's eyes that made me think she was older than us, fifty maybe, the clingy velour suit could have been on the body of a twenty-five-year-old. Her face was wrinkle-free, even when she smiled.

A black Lexus stopped at the foot of the driveway. The driver lowered his window. "Ahoy! Welcome to the neighborhood."

"Speak of the devil." Kristen motioned him up the driveway. "Come say a proper hello!"

He reversed, then pulled up next to us and stepped out of the car, leaving the door open and the engine running. The air conditioning clung to him like a cloud.

"Johnny, this is Kurt and Maggie." Kristen reached behind him and shut the door to silence the beeping. The top of her head reached to Johnny's armpit. With his graying temples and paunch, he looked more like her father than her husband.

His hand was cold. "She tell you about Trolleyween?"

"For heaven's sake, Johnny, that's not for months. You'd think that was the only thing we do for fun around here."

Johnny pulled up his jeans and spread his feet a little wider. "Halloween for grownups." He winked at Maggie. A winker. I leaned closer to Maggie. "We rent a trolley that drives us around the subdivision. This year, it's the odd-numbered houses' turn to provide the—" he paused, "—treats." He checked out the number on our mailbox. "Looks like you guys get to be 'trickers' this year."

"Yeah, yeah. And we're on for *treats*. Anyway, ours is the taupe house on the corner of Huckleberry and Twin Oaks, next to the double lot. If you need anything—"

"That'll be quite an introduction to the neighborhood!" Johnny chuckled. "Start thinking about your costumes now."

Kristen put her hand on her husband's arm. "You think he's a little proud of his little trolley-brainchild?" She smiled but it was hard to tell if she meant it. "We should get out of their hair, Johnny. They've got unpacking to do." She started toward the car. "Let's not make it Halloween before we see each other again, okay?"

Maggie held up the plate. "Thanks again for the popovers!"

Kristen's comment about not seeing each other until Halloween wasn't an exaggeration. We seldom saw any neighbors except for Saturday afternoons when the husbands mowed their lawns simultaneously. I'd jump on our rider mower when the first guy got out there, hoping one of them would wave me over for a beer after we finished, but, when we were done, the lawns cleared just as quickly as they'd filled with mowers.

Getting to know the neighbors wasn't any easier for Maggie, who complained about how far apart the mailboxes were and how the women seemed always to be going somewhere dressed in fashionable workout clothes or out-to-lunch pantsuits. She felt like a kid on the edge of a playground waiting to be invited into the kickball game. When I'd ask her if she thought moving was a mistake, though, she would insist she had no regrets and touch her stomach for good luck. "I'm keeping my eyes on the prize."

By the Fourth of July, we were more than ready for some familiar faces and invited our families for a cookout. My mom and sister, Robin, were the only two who could make it. Without the buffer of nieces, nephews and in-laws around, Robin was a little less on her best behavior than usual.

"Now tell the truth, brother." She pulled two beers from the cooler, opened them and handed one to me. "How's life in Stepford?"

The question was so typical of Robin: gush all over the new house while Maggie gave her the grand tour, then drop the "Now-tell-the-truth" question while Maggie and Mom assembled the dessert inside.

I took a swig and finished running the wire brush over the grill grate.

"Let's just say it's nice not to wake up to the neighbor's alarm at five o'clock every morning."

"I thought he was a drug dealer."

"No, the neighbor on the other side. The OCD guy who painted his roof white." Thinking about our old neighbors made me glad we'd taken the leap even though we weren't positive we could make the stretch financially. So far, so good.

"When we first moved here it was so quiet I felt like I had cotton in my ears. Now, I'm used to it. Sleep like a baby."

Robin snorted. "That's all you got? It's quiet and you sleep well?" I tried to think of a way to turn the conversation but came up short. "You must really hate it here."

"No." The word came out before she'd finished her sentence. "I don't hate it. It's actually nice to come home to quiet. Relax on the deck. Watch the birds. I've had enough excitement for one life."

We both knew the excitement I'd referred to was named Jocelyn. Jocelyn of the turbulent argument, of the hot make-up sex, of the bipolar episodes that made life with her thrilling and exhausting at the same time. Through common friends, Robin knew way more about our relationship than a little sister should. Including Jocelyn's Hepatitis C diagnosis a month after we'd broken up for good. Compared to the "excitement" of waiting for test results to determine whether I'd contracted an incurable, liver-devouring illness, a good night's sleep was appealing.

"I'll drink to that!" Robin clinked my bottle.

"Drink to what?" Maggie held a glass dessert pan with blueberries, strawberries and whipped cream in the form of an American flag. She tried to balance it while she opened the sliding screen door.

Robin turned to face me and mouthed, "Step-ford," then opened the door for Maggie. "We were drinking to how nice and quiet your new neighborhood is. That dessert is gorgeous, Maggie." She dropped her beer bottle into the recycling bin. "When did you get so—domestic?"

Maggie blushed. "Oh, I've always liked little touches like this. Since I'm not working, I actually have the time to make things nice."

I took a swig of beer, so I wouldn't have to see Robin's reaction to the news that Maggie had quit her job.

"Yeah, did Maggie tell you?" Mom stepped onto the deck closing the sliding screen door behind her. "She's not at the daycare anymore. Too long a commute. Besides, she and Kurt are trying to get pregnant."

"Mother, Kurt can try all he wants. *He's* never going to get pregnant." Robin turned to Maggie. "Doesn't it drive you nuts when men say, '*We're* pregnant?' It's all the woman's show, you ask me."

"I'd be so happy to be pregnant," Maggie said, "I wouldn't care how Kurt talked about it." The pan started to tip forward like she was losing her grip.

Mom reached for the dessert. "Here, let me take that." She scowled at Robin. "Maggie *will* get pregnant *soon*, and then," she lifted her chin my way, "Kurt will be so involved and supportive it'll feel like they're sharing the pregnancy." She thumped the pan on the table. "I must've left the spatula on the counter."

Like a sassy teenager, Robin widened her eyes at Mom's back. But then she saw Maggie's face. "Gosh, I'm sorry. I didn't know it was such a tender subject."

"No, that's okay. The doctor said it might take up to a year."

"Yeah, I've heard it can take a while to get the pill out of your system."

Maggie looked confused. "The pill? I've never been on the pill."

"No? Well, it's none of my business."

Mom opened the kitchen window. "Maggie, honey? Do you remember where you put the spatula? I don't see it anywhere."

"I'll help you look."

Robin waited until she'd closed the screen door. "Now tell the truth—"

"Don't even."

"No, seriously, if she wasn't on the pill, what were you guys—?"

"None of your business."

"Let me guess: she wanted to leave it up to God."

I kept my mouth shut.

"That's the same as *trying* if you ask me."

I considered this. If she was right, we'd have grounds to request fertility testing sooner than later. After the stories I'd heard from other guys at work about the fertility rigmarole their wives had gone through, though, I was in no hurry to let that genie out of the bottle. The worst was Mario's wife who gave herself shots in the stomach for months and still couldn't carry a pregnancy to term. Not to mention the cost. Mario was still writing checks to the clinic with no baby to show for it.

"Maybe you're shooting blanks."

Robin's comment reminded me why I avoided spending time with her. She always managed to run her fingernails across my skin and pick a scab I didn't know was there.

I took the top off the grill and started scraping the grate with a wire brush even though it was already clean. If I was shooting blanks, what about Jocelyn's pregnancy? Talk about dodging a bullet. Of course, there was no telling how many guys she'd slept with while we had been "off again." I closed the grill's vents and rolled it closer to the house.

Mom slid the screen door open and waved the spatula. "I left it in the pantry. Why I took it in there, I'll never know."

I picked up the grilling utensils and dirty platter and headed into the house. Let Mom and Maggie deal with Robin for awhile.

The rest of summer passed quietly. We tended our small vegetable garden, painted the kitchen and fell asleep to the call of a katydid outside our bedroom window every night. We exchanged friendly waves as the neighbors drove past our driveway and, once in awhile, yelled a comment across the street about the weather. Maggie soon learned the best prospect for socializing was to bump into someone at the grocery store.

One day in early September, she returned with an armload of groceries and excitement in her voice. "Did you know the Birenkotts have eight kids? Can you believe it? Eight."

Who were the Birenkotts? Maggie was practically breathless filling me in on the details, as if their fertility were contagious. All girls, each of them eighteen months apart. The neighborhood had nicknamed them The Rabbit Family. "All in good fun, of course."

I tried to imagine the path of the conversation among the cantaloupes or in the soup aisle that had led to this piece of information, then decided I didn't care. It was nice to see Maggie so enthused.

"They send the kids to their grandparents' for Trolley-ween." Ah, *those* Birenkotts. "They split them up. Four for each set." She moved the milk to the other side of the refrigerator. "Maybe I'll sew our costumes. Kristen says people go all out." She folded the grocery bags and turned on the computer. It wasn't long before she was cutting fabric and sewing seams. I silently hoped the project would distract Maggie from her obsession with getting pregnant. It didn't.

"Dear Lord," Maggie folded her hands and closed her eyes.

I slid out the little pillow from under the bed and tucked it under my knees. When it was my night to offer the prayer, my knees could take it: a quick recap of the day, a few things we were grateful for, blessings for loved ones, and, of course, the assurance we'd lovingly accept a new soul entrusted to our care when He saw fit to bless us with a baby. Amen.

Maggie's prayers, however, seemed to be getting longer with each passing day. "Thank you for these wonderful months in our new home and please shower the Millers with your blessings."

Weeks earlier, I had stopped mentioning the Millers in my prayers. Certainly, the family was back on their feet by now. Besides, when I stopped praying for them, the burning sensation in my chest went away. I could probably thank the reflux medicine for that, but you never know.

"Lord, thank you for leading me to the *Fertility Now!* website where I can read stories of others who had trouble conceiving, just like us."

I thought of the unopened SpermCheck home fertility test in the glove compartment of my car. The fire in my chest was back.

Maggie was giving God a recap of the stories she'd read on *Fertility Now!* Across the bed, I could sense her chest filling with hope.

"I trust you, dear Lord, but if we are not meant to conceive in the usual way, thank you for leading me to *Fertility Now!* so I can learn how many different ways there are to conceive a child. Amen."

She cleared her throat. I opened my eyes. She was staring at me.

"Amen."

Her expression reminded me that there was a star drawn on today's date on the calendar: the optimal day for conceiving. I forced a smile and tried to look horny. I pushed myself up from the floor and slid the pillow back under the bed.

"I'll be right back."

I closed the bathroom door and rummaged in the bottom of the towel closet. I knew it was a risk to keep the Playboy lingerie issue tucked between two beach towels in the back, but it was the only thing that had allowed me to get it up for weeks. I'd decided if Maggie found it and got upset, I'd just tell her I was picturing *her* in the lingerie. And, really, that wasn't so far from the truth. I couldn't remember the last time she'd worn anything even the slightest bit alluring, but I could always conjure up the memory of our wedding night. The simple powder blue spaghetti-strap, what had she called it, a cami? It came just to her hips and gave me tiny peeks at what she jokingly called her "forbidden fruit" with each step she took toward me, waiting on the hotel bed. My hard-on had raged. I didn't buy any of the talk about secondary virginity that women mentioned in their *ChristianMingle.com* profiles, but after a year of abstinence following Jocelyn and another two years of it while Maggie and I had dated, our wedding night did feel like I was about to experience sex for the first time.

"Are you coming?"

I pushed her muffled voice out of my mind and held onto the picture of her lifting her knee to climb onto the king-sized bed, giving me peeks of cleavage and outlines of erect nipples. I opened our bathroom door. She lay on her side, propping her head on her hand. Her hair looked a little extra fluffed, and her lips were shiny. Was that mascara on her eyelashes?

She checked out my hard-on. "Thinking about me?"

Grateful to tell the truth, I smiled. "Yup." But what she wore wasn't right. It looked silky, but pink with lace trim that would feel scratchy when my skin brushed against it. I tried to stay focused on her desire to please me. I'd just have to close my eyes and be careful where I put my hands.

I knew a blow job or doggie style would be too much to hope for—Maggie wouldn't let us risk wasting any sperm when she was in the ovulating window—but I took a chance and lifted the satin over her head and dribbled a line of kisses down her front until I reached her crotch. I gently opened her legs.

She let out a small, "Oh." And then, "This is going to be the time, I just know it."

With those words, I felt my own window closing. I stopped mid-lick and pushed into her. I came with one thrust.

A confused look crossed Maggie's face. Then she found herself. "Quick, stick a pillow under my hips." I did as I was told and went to the bathroom to clean up.

One more ovulation cycle and it was time for Trolley-ween. I had to admit, I was looking forward to an excuse to let loose a little, break the ice with the other guys in the neighborhood, forget about getting pregnant. I didn't even care that I looked like an idiot in my over-sized Little Boy Blue overalls, straw hat and shoes with enormous buckles.

When I came downstairs, Maggie's face looked like she was about to throw up.

"What's the matter? Did Little Bo Peep lose her sheep?"

Sitting on the ottoman with her ruffled hoop skirt spread around her, Maggie stared at the little plastic stick in her hand. The results of my own in-home test, the one I had taken that morning, knocked on the door of my conscience: sub-fertile sperm count which may cause inability to conceive.

She said, "I know. I know. We've only been trying for seven months, but I'm starting to think I can't get pregnant at all."

"Aw, Mags, don't say that now." I should have told her that most likely it was my low sperm count to blame. That would have been the kind thing to do. But I didn't feel like being kind. "Look on the bright side."

Her face questioned what could possibly be "bright" about this situation.

"Well, yeah." I tried to make my voice light. The trolley would be here any minute. "Since you're *not* pregnant, you can have a few drinks, really enjoy yours—"

"Seriously?! I should be glad I'm not pregnant so I can *drink* tonight?"

As it came out, I knew it was a jerky thing to say, but I couldn't stop myself.

She stood up and grabbed her shepherd's hook. For a second, I thought she was going to hit me with it. She took a breath to speak but was interrupted by the clang of the trolley bell, then two short beeps.

I knew I should apologize but tried for logic instead. "I'm just saying, by this time next year, we'll have a little one," my chest caught with the lie, "and we won't even *want* to join Trolleyween. We might as well enjoy it while we don't have the responsibility of a baby." At the word, "responsibility," she turned on her heel and marched toward the door. "Here's our chance to get to know the neighbors better," I said to an empty room.

We sat in the third seat of the trolley not touching. You had to hand it to these people. They certainly went all out for Halloween. Tarzan and Jane, the Conways from down the street, boarded the trolley looking like they had spent time in the tanning bed in preparation for the evening. Or maybe they had actually gone somewhere tropical.

They carried travel mugs and spoke in fragmented sentences. "Tarzan drink! Jane drink, too!" They clinked cups and found a seat. I could have sworn they were wearing real animal skins.

I tried a joke. "You think she got a boob job just for the occasion?" Maggie usually smiled when I made fun of the Conways from afar. No dice.

Next we picked up Stephanie and Pete, who didn't look like they were dressed in costume, although Stephanie wore a tiny sequined dress whose neckline plunged to her navel.

"Who you? Kardashian?" yelled Tarzan from the back of the trolley.

Stephanie blew him a little kiss. "You got that right! Anybody guess who Pete is?"

The trolley was quiet for a second. The driver ventured a guess. "That guy in *Wolf of Wall Street*?"

"Close, my friend!" Pete held up his own travel mug.

As far as I could tell, these were the clothes Pete wore to work every day at the brokerage firm.

"I'm the One-Percent!" Pete pointed at Tarzan. "You there, you stinking hippie. Got a problem with me. Get a job why don'tcha?"

If he'd have been a buddy from work, I would have taken his words as satire, but he was serious. Not only was the costume offensive, but it was out of date. He'd have to explain who he was supposed to be all night long, and people would have to laugh politely, like it was the cleverest thing they'd heard all day.

"Looks like these guys have a head start on us," I said.

"Yeah," she whispered, "good thing I'm not pregnant, so I can catch up with them."

Soon we were walking up to Kristen and Johnny's porch. The door was already open, and Kristen held a tray of martini glasses enveloped in a cloud of swirling smoke. The liquid was a red so deep it was almost black.

"Trick or treat!" We helped ourselves to glasses and walked into the warm living room that smelled like cinnamon.

Kristen wore sparkly red horns, a shiny red dress and spiked high heels that made her nearly as tall as me. "Careful. There's dry ice at the bottom. Drink slow-ly."

I turned to clink glasses with Maggie but she was too far away to reach.

Kristen lifted her glass and touched mine lightly, then said to the room. "Here's to it!"

We lifted our glasses to our hostess who glanced toward the wide, curving staircase.

Johnny's voice bellowed from the top of the stairs. "Thou shalt not covet thy neighbor's wife!" He wore a flowing robe with a gold rope belt, sandals and a long, wavy blonde wig and a beard to match.

"Hey there, Moses!" The One-Percent called to him.

"Moses?!" Johnny pointed his staff at Pete. "I smite you!"

Kristen rolled her eyes. "He's God. Get it? I'm Satan. He's God. I told him no one would get it." She finished what was left in her glass and said so only I could hear,

"I think he just likes the idea of smiting people all night."

God made his way through the crowd, slapping backs and bestowing blessings. When he got to Maggie, he noticed her empty glass and handed her another. She caught my eye and held up her glass. Her expression told me to be careful what I wished for.

The trolley sounded its bell.

"Thou shalt board the trolley!" God commanded.

By the time we'd sampled all the other treats of the odd-numbered neighbors and headed toward the Birenkotts', I was grateful for the large yards and many cul-de-sacs. Not quite as many houses to trick-or-treat at as I'd thought. I stared at the side of Maggie's head trying to get her to look at me. I reached for her hand, but she slipped it under her thigh.

The trolley bell clanged as we pulled into a circular driveway. The Birenkotts lived at the highest point of the subdivision. Their house couldn't be called a mansion, but I figured it would probably sell for ten times my salary. At least.

Maggie slipped into the crowded aisle and was out of the trolley before I could get out of our row.

"Have fun now!" The driver closed the door and pulled away.

As he drove away, it occurred to me we'd have no way home. I turned and looked in the direction of our house. A mile and a half at least, in pinchy big-buckled shoes, dressed like a nursery rhyme.

"Don't worry," Kristen's voice surprised me. "He'll be back around two to take people home," she said. "Come on. Let's see what treats the Birenkotts have for us." She strutted toward the house, her devil tail bouncing along behind her.

Kristen pointed out our hosts, who were already engaged in conversation with other guests. Mrs. Birenkott wore the elaborate wig and geisha-type makeup of Padme in the *Star Wars* prequel movies. Her husband was the spitting image of Supreme Chancellor Palpatine.

I took a glass of champagne from a passing waiter's tray, then noticed Maggie, across the living room laughing with Tarzan. I grabbed an extra glass and headed her direction.

Before I could get to her, God clapped his hand on my shoulder.

"Some party, huh?" There was no getting around his bulk. "Two fisting it?"

"Bottom's up!" I lifted one glass and drained it, then caught sight of Palpatine clinking glasses with Maggie. I polished off the second glass.

"Atta boy!" God laughed. "Tell you what. You like bourbon?" He didn't wait for me to answer. "Birenkott is a bourbon connoisseur. Let's go up to his study and sample his latest discovery." When he led with his staff, he really did look like Moses, as the revelers stepped aside to make way for us.

I closed out the party sounds behind the heavy oak door. I wasn't one to drink hard liquor, but I could tell it was important for Johnny to impress me even if it was with another man's bourbon. Following his lead, I held the glass up to the light, swirled the amber liquid, and took a deep whiff before taking a sip. I followed his advice to hold liquor on my tongue before swallowing.

"Ah, now isn't that something?"

He was right. The bourbon didn't trip my gag reflex like the shot of Jack Daniels had on my twenty-first birthday. Now I knew why people used the word "smooth" to describe fine liquor. Smooth and warm.

We sipped the bourbon, the bassline of the music down stairs like a hypnotic heartbeat. Before I knew it, he was pouring another.

"So, you and Maggie been married long?"

When I told him only two years, he looked disappointed. "You're practically still on your honeymoon then."

The word "hardly" came out of my mouth before I could stop it.

"Really? Things seemed pretty good when you moved in."

I had no idea how he could tell anything about Maggie and me from our conversation on moving day. As I remembered it, neither Maggie nor I had gotten a word in edgewise, and all he could talk about was Trolleyween. The more I thought about it, the more it seemed that Trolleyween was the cause of Maggie's iciness tonight. It felt good to aim the blame at Johnny and his childish trick-or-treat party.

"Yeah, well." I could hear an edge in my voice and stopped.

The One-Percent tapped on the door as he opened it. "You beat me to it." Johnny grabbed a fresh glass and poured.

I stood up. "Good timing. You can take my seat. Is the bathroom this way?"

Johnny nodded. "Nice drinking with you."

"Same here. Thanks."

I took my place in line for the bathroom and steadied myself against the wall. Looking back at me was a portrait of The Rabbit Family. I had to admit, there was a certain rabbity quality to them. Maybe because they looked like Easter eggs in their pastel polos. Maybe because they had pinched little noses. Birenkott—I hadn't heard anyone use his first name—had a healthy glow and a broad smile. He was the clear focal point of the photograph with the eight children surrounding him like rays of the sun, their faces tilted the slightest bit toward their father. Each of the children had his sharp jawline and fair hair. I wondered if Mrs. Birenkott, the only one with brown hair and a normal-sized nose, felt like an interloper positioned behind her husband's left shoulder.

I took out my phone and pretended to check emails while the women ahead of me reminisced about Trolleyweens past. When it was my turn, I took longer in the bathroom than I should have. I breathed long, slow breaths and drank water out of my cupped hands in hopes of sobering up. I decided to find Maggie. It was time to go home, even if we had to walk.

I headed for the lower level. The kitschy Halloween music that had been playing earlier had switched to smooth jazz. In the dim light, I could see the Conways slow dancing in the corner, Tarzan with his hand on Jane's ass, Jane probing his ear with her tongue.

I scanned the room for Maggie. Maybe she was getting a tour of the house or had fallen asleep in one of the bedrooms. Maybe I could find her and we could curl up together until the trolley came back for us.

"The neighborhood likes to let loose for Trolleyween. I hope we haven't made you regret buying the Millers' house." Kristen held out a full glass of champagne.

"Huh?" I tried to think of a way to refuse the glass but couldn't. I pretended to take a sip. "No, we love the house."

"I noticed Maggie's drinking. I guess that means no baby." It seemed a cruel thing to say, but her eyes looked sympathetic. She touched my forearm lightly. "Yet, of course. *Yet.*"

"Not if it's up to me." I had meant it as a joke, but the truth of it stung.

"Oh, geez. I put my foot in it *again.*" She polished off her champagne. "Sometimes I swear if there's a wrong thing to say, I'll say it."

"No, it's okay. I was trying to be funny. It didn't work." I took a swallow of champagne to show her I was still having a good time.

She lowered her voice. "Don't tell Johnny I told you this, but it took a long time to conceive Ben. A *really* long time." She was standing so close I could see the glitter in her mascara. "I found a way. Maggie will, too."

I scanned the room for Johnny. While the smiting thing had been funny for a while, I didn't want to incur the wrath of God just then. I closed my eyes and concentrated on my breathing.

"Are you okay?"

I tried to smile. "Yeah, I'm just not used to drinking this much."

"I know just the thing. Come with me."

I followed her down a hallway and out through a sliding door to the biggest hot tub I'd ever seen. Six people were soaking, holding their drinks above the effervescence, all still wearing their masks and wigs, and, it took me a beat to realize it, the women weren't wearing bathing suits. I double-checked the backs of heads for Maggie's ringlets half hoping she was among them, then feeling relief that she wasn't.

There was God, his smiting stick propped against the house, his curly beard soaked and clinging to his hairy chest. A feather from the Las Vegas showgirl's peacock headdress had found its way into his wig. She looked down at her breasts as if checking to make sure they were still there. Next to her, Martin Mortenson in his Harry Potter glasses and lightning bolt scar sat shirtless with his Hogwarts tie floating on the water's surface. He was talking timeshares in Cabo with Pete. Catching sight of Kristen, Stephanie slid closer to her husband.

"Ah, Satan." God beckoned. "Come join us in the Holy Soak. Play your cards right, and I'll let you back into Heaven."

Kristen kicked off her heels. After two years of watching Maggie undress, awkwardly, as if she was ashamed, I'd forgotten not all women undressed that way. Kristen slid her body-hugging dress onto the deck like she was peeling a banana. She wasn't wearing underwear. She glanced at me, not in seductiveness I was sure—with her husband right there—but to challenge me. "Perfect hangover preventive."

She stepped up the stairs and lowered her right foot into the water. In my quick glimpse, I could tell two things about her body. She worked out. Hard. And she didn't have a lick of body hair. Anywhere. I wondered what it would feel like to make love to her.

God's booming voice made me jump. "How about you, Boy Blue?"

"Yeah, take my place." Martin stood up confirming the men were naked, too.

I held up my hand, grateful for my baggy overalls masking the beginnings of a hard-on. "Oh, not me. I can't swim." I hoped they'd appreciate my levity and let me off the hook.

"Aw, don't be a party pooper." God slid himself under his wife and placed both hands on her breasts. "Go find that sweet bride of yours and join us." He switched to his Mount Sinai voice. "I command it!"

Grateful for the excuse to escape, I headed back into the house to find Maggie.

Palpatine passed me on the stairs. A grin played on his face like he had just vanquished the Galactic Republic. "You getting enough to drink there, Boy Blue? Your hands are empty."

I held them up like I was under arrest. "I've had plenty." I was about to introduce myself but was interrupted by someone yelling up the stairs asking how to change the music. I said, "Great party, thank you," to his back.

When I couldn't find Maggie in the vast kitchen or the family room, I headed to the second floor and quietly opened bedroom doors hoping to find her napping among a pile of jackets or talking about drapes with Mrs. Birenkott. I thought about all the parties I'd left by myself when Jocelyn would up and disappear or tell me

she wasn't done partying and I should go on home without her. In fact, that was one of the first things I loved
about dating Maggie: we always left a party together.

I looked at my watch. The trolley would be back in a
half-hour to take us home. I couldn't think of anything
I wanted more. Our quiet bed in our quiet house.

The door of the last room had a construction paper
sign that said, "Madeline's Room. Do NOT Enter. This
means YOU!" The butterflies and rainbows made me
wonder just how serious Madeline's warning was. I pictured a similar sign on the door of one of our bedrooms
and realized how much Maggie would love having a
child. Not just the baby she was obsessed with now, but
a little boy or girl she could push on a swing or teach
letters and colors—all the things she had been doing
for other people's children for years. She deserved that.
I wanted to give it to her.

I turned the knob slowly. Maggie was perched on a
princess bedspread with her back to the door. In her
puffy-sleeved costume, she looked right at home on the
canopy bed surrounded by pink walls. I thought about
sliding behind her and gently putting my hands over
her eyes. *Guess who's sorry?* I'd say and kiss her neck.
Let's go home.

I was about to step into the room when I noticed her
bloomers in a bunch on the floor. My first inclination
was to close the door, turn my back on what I knew had
happened. Maybe I would go back to the hot tub and
see if I could seduce Kristen while God was parting
someone else's Red Sea.

Before I could close the door, though, the music got loud and Maggie turned around. I could see the regret on her face even before it registered that I was standing there. She hesitated, then walked around the bed and stood in front of me with her head bowed. "I am so sorry," she managed to say. "Can you ever forgive me?"

No excuses. No blowing it off as nothing. No attempt to blame me. Just an apology and the opportunity to forgive. I was tempted to say, "I'm done forgiving women for being unfaithful." But I had never actually forgiven Jocelyn for anything. She had never asked. After each infidelity, I had simply taken her back and pretended that nothing had happened. Besides, Maggie wasn't Jocelyn. She was my wife. We had pledged a lifetime to each other, and Maggie's bent head and drooping shoulders told me this would be her first, last, and only infidelity for that lifetime. I thought of my own little secret, the one I should have told her before we ever boarded that stupid trolley. Only I would never get the guts to tell her the truth. I would end up holding onto that secret—and the guilt that went with it—for the rest of our marriage.

Neither of us could know that our desperate attempts to conceive were over, that nine months later, Maggie would give birth to a daughter who looked enough like me that even I couldn't be sure she hadn't been conceived in the first, tender love-making of forgiveness.

I picked up the bloomers and stuffed them into my pocket. Maggie's apology waited. I knew I would forgive her—had already forgiven her in fact—but I couldn't say the words just yet. I reached for her hand.

"We need to get out of here."

Nothing to Lose

The day after Ricardo the mailman carried away her application for disability, Marilou decided it was time to take control. Of course, she couldn't give up chocolate altogether. But, if she made herself follow every bit of wisdom printed inside the wrapper of each Dove candy, her progress to the bottom of the bag could be slowed significantly.

Especially if they were all like the message on the first wrapper of The Dove Vow: *Dance like no one is watching*. Marilou glued the wrapper into her journal and wrote, "June 7, 1994: Marilou takes The Dove Vow."

It took her the better part of the morning to build up enough courage to push herself off the couch, turn on Q106 and do her best line dance to "Boot Scootin' Boogie." The scuff turn was tough, and she nearly took a tumble when her shin hit the end table. She knew she didn't look anything like those skinny young girls on the Brooks & Dunn video, but it felt good to move her body anyway. She did her heel-toe, do-si-do and crooned, "Come on, baby, let's go."

She was tempted to close the curtains—her living room looked right onto Main Street after all—but she knew a *private* dance for "no one" was not the intent of the words. In order to eat the candy, she needed to live up to the spirit of the advice, not just the letter of it. With sweat beads on her upper lip, she'd almost finished the entire song when she stole a glance out the window and saw a flash of blue on her front stoop. Her stomach dropped.

Ricardo lifted her mail in greeting, a shy smile on his face. She could see the red ascending from his chin to his bald pate. To heck with the chocolate. She snapped off the radio and reached out the screen door. "Thanks, Ricardo," she managed to cough out before retreating behind the door.

She spent the rest of the day building up for another dance for "no one" but never could bring herself to do it. Into the trash went her Dove.

The next day, the wrapper's advice was not much easier to execute. *Share a chocolate moment with a new friend.* She read it twice as she neatly folded the corners of the foil so they looked like arrows pointing to the message and tried to think of who the new "friend" might be.

Another flash of blue and the sound of envelopes landing on the floor. She didn't blame Ricardo for slipping the mail through the slot in her door after the awkward dancing incident yesterday. Marilou could taste the smooth, creamy chocolate on her tongue. She felt a tingle between her legs.

"Ricardo!" She yelled and toddled to the door. "Wait a second."

He stopped at the bottom of the steps and turned slowly.

"Do you like chocolate?"

His face turned the color of canned ham. "Chocolate?"

"Yes, I'd like to give you a chocolate." She stepped onto the stoop and held out the bag, so he could choose one.

"That is very kind." He thanked her and ripped the candy's red foil. Marilou resisted the urge to tell him to be careful, that there was a fortune inside, but she reminded herself it was she who had taken the pledge, not Ricardo.

He looked around for a place to discard the wrapper. Marilou held out her hand. "I'll take care of that for you." She held up her own chocolate as if it were a glass of wine. "Cheers!" They clinked candies and ate them.

"Mmm. Delicious. Thank you, Marilou." He cleared his throat. "Well, I'd better go." He walked down the three stairs.

"Ricardo, wait—"

He stole a glance at his watch. "Yes?"

She had nothing to tell him, but she didn't want him to leave either. "Thanks. For stopping." She could think of nothing else. "You probably have a schedule to keep. Don't let me hold you up."

"That's okay." He walked backwards toward the main sidewalk. "Thanks again. For the chocolate."

It might have been Marilou's imagination, but she could have sworn he had a spring in his step as he headed toward the neighbors' house. She closed the door, flattened out his wrapper and pushed together a rip so she could read the advice: *Look for love in unexpected places*. She stuck his wrapper next to hers and wrote, "Ricardo's Wrapper, June 8, 1994."

Her advice for the next few days was a mix of easy and hard-to-do. *Enjoy the silky smoothness of Dove* and *Happiness is just one bite away* did nothing for her intention to limit her chocolate intake. On the other hand, she didn't see how she would be able to *Do something for someone less fortunate today*. How could anyone be less fortunate than her? She was almost at the end of her unemployment benefits, she had no prospects for work, and her only remaining option had been to apply for disability—"going on the dole," her father would have called it. He was probably rolling over in his grave.

She tried to shake the memory of a childhood of listening to his rants against the lazy moochers on welfare and her fear that he would quit work and join them, just to make a point. "I'll quit putting in my forty hours," he would threaten, "send you to the foodbank, Marilou. 'Oh, poor me,' you'll say, and they'll give you cornmeal and canned beans to bring home for supper."

Her mother said he was bluffing, but Marilou had believed him. She thought of all the years she had spent afraid of becoming poor, the shame of welfare hanging over her head. The years of hoarding food, first in her closet, then in her own body. She'd never had to ask for a handout. Until now.

After two-and-a-half days of trying to come up with someone who had it worse than her, she remembered her Uncle Orv in the last stages of Alzheimer's. She considered taking him some chocolates at the home, but, when she opened *Sing along with the elevator music,* she saved herself the trouble and tossed both chocolates and their wrappers into the trash.

One afternoon, when she returned from her tour of the neighborhood—*Walk your way to happiness!* and *Go farther than you think you can!*—she collapsed onto the couch and lifted her feet out in front of her to assess the two angry red blisters where her flip-flops had rubbed. She thought about getting herself a bucket of soapy water for foot soaking but, considering the effort it would take, decided to follow her mother's favorite cure: let the air get at it. And, while she was listening to her mother, she followed her advice about the telephone that was now ringing in the kitchen: let it ring.

When she couldn't stand the shrill of it any longer, she pushed herself from the couch. It was Sharon, full of complaints. Why didn't Marilou get an answering machine? And worries. She'd called twice in the last half-hour, and it just rang and rang. If Marilou hadn't picked up this time, she was about to get in her car and drive right over. Or send the police.

Marilou wedged the receiver between her shoulder and ear and stretched for the open bag of candy on the counter. She popped a chocolate into her mouth without stopping to read the wrapper.

"Anyway, the reason I'm calling is, guess who won four free tickets to—" she made a snare drum sound with her tongue, "see Billy Ray Cyrus in Rockford!" She made a woo-hoo sound. "Can you believe it?"

Marilou started to answer, but Sharon cut her off. "They're $25 face value, so I figure we can sell the other two and treat ourselves to a nice dinner somewhere beforehand. What do you think?" This time she stopped long enough for Marilou to respond.

As Marilou fiddled with the wrapper, she answered with questions of her own. Weren't they too old to go to a concert? When was it anyway? What about the drive? All that way and at night, too? Besides, what would she even wear?

"Listen to you." Sharon laughed. "It's like you've never been to a concert before."

Marilou didn't want to tell Sharon that, yes, going to a concert was one of the many, many things she had never done before, that she'd never been on a date, that the only man she'd ever danced with was her uncle. She smoothed the wrapper on the table in front of her. *Dare to do what you've never done before.*

There was no turning back now. Marilou had already eaten the chocolate; now she had to follow the advice. She took a deep breath and looked around the kitchen.

"Can you hold on a minute, Sharon? I've got something on the stove." She set the receiver on the table and stared at it. It was preposterous to even consider asking Ricardo on a date. Still, at this very moment, it was the only thing she dared to want to do. When you've got nothing to lose, you've got nothing to lose, she thought. They should put *that* on a Dove wrapper.

She picked up the receiver. "Can I buy the third ticket, too? I want to invite someone along." The phone was silent. "Sharon? You there?"

"What? Yeah, I'm here." Sharon's smile seeped into her voice. "You got a boyfriend or something?"

Marilou squared her shoulders, steadied her voice. "Not a boyfriend, but I would like to invite—" she made her own drum roll, "a man." The conversation continued with a complaint. *You didn't tell me you were interested in someone!* And a question. *Who is he?*

"Look, there's no guarantee he'll even say yes—"

"Tell you what. If he's got a friend for me, you've got a deal."

Marilou sat on the edge of her La-Z-Boy, feet firm on the floor ready to carry her to the door the moment she saw Ricardo coming up the walk.

Her shoes pinched. The waistband on her slacks hugged her right under her ribcage and reminded her how long it had been since she'd had to dress for work. But today demanded more than a loose cotton dress. Today called for a blouse and a touch of blush. Lipstick, of course. And perfume.

The longer she sat, the more certain she became that the notion of inviting Ricardo was ridiculous. It was those gosh-darned chocolates. They were the trouble. When she could stand the waiting no longer, she lifted herself from the chair and grabbed the Dove bag from the end table. She would take it to the outside garbage can and get rid of them once and for all. Join Weight Watchers or something.

She opened the door just as Ricardo leaned to slip a letter through the mail slot.

"Oh." She heard her voice but wasn't sure it was she who had spoken. "Marilou."

Ricardo straightened up and held out the envelope, its return address marked Social Security Administration. She grabbed her purse from the entryway table and shoved the letter inside. Maybe he hadn't noticed who it was from.

He motioned to the candy bag. "Careful," he winked, "I'm liable to get addicted."

She was puzzled at first but then Marilou realized he thought she was offering him a chocolate. She held out the bag.

His smile showed a dimple in his left cheek. "Don't mind if I do!" Ricardo adjusted the strap of his mail pouch and reached into the bag. Again, he handed her the wrapper and ate the heart-shaped chocolate in two bites.

Marilou glanced at his fortune: *Wear that perfect dress tonight!* She tried not to grin as she pictured Ricardo in a dress. "Do you like music, Ricardo?"

He tilted his head and looked to her left, as if that was where the question had come from. "To tell you the truth, the only kind I can stand is—" He looked over his shoulder, and she half-hoped he'd say Classical or Rock 'n Roll or Mariachi to give his inevitable rejection less sting. "—Country. Why?"

"I have an extra ticket to see Billy Ray Cyrus in Rockford," she blurted before she had a chance to lose her nerve.

"Really? A ticket to see him live?"

She nodded.

He put down his mailbag and reached into his back pocket. "How much is the ticket?" He opened his wallet and thumbed through the bills inside.

"Oh." Marilou realized she had said it all wrong. "No, no." Goodness, this was difficult. "I'm asking—" How could she clarify? "—inviting you to come along—" she paused, "with my friend, Sharon, and me. You could bring a friend." Now she needed to make sure there was no confusion. "My treat. A double date." There.

Ricardo looked at her forehead, then at his shoes. His facial expression changed as if it were having a conversation that only he could hear. He bit the inside of his cheek.

The silence lasted so long, Marilou became conscious of a jackhammer pounding down the street. Or maybe that was her heart.

Ricardo's eyes glinted as he slipped his wallet back into his pocket. "Well, chocolate *and* a ticket to see Billy Ray Cyrus with a pretty lady. I'm just about the luckiest mailman alive today!"

Marilou nearly hugged him. She had been so worried about getting turned down that she'd never considered the possibility he'd accept, much less appreciate it and call her a "pretty lady." Talk about being lucky to be alive.

Marilou left the letter from Social Security in the bottom of her purse. She couldn't prepare for her first date knowing she had a "disability," couldn't think about all the pity on Ricardo's face when he would deliver her disability checks. *Worry wastes wisdom!*

Sharon took her on a shopping spree at the *Farm and Fleet* to buy an outfit for the concert. When Marilou tried on a suede vest, Sharon gushed, "Put that over a white blouse and a denim skirt, and you'll look just like someone on *Dance Ranch!*" Marilou drew the line at buying a straw cowboy hat but couldn't resist the tan cowboy boots on the clearance rack. Flip-flops just wouldn't cut it.

She tried on the outfit daily, practiced walking in the boots, swishing the skirt just a little. By the time the day of the concert arrived, she no longer felt like an imposter in the clothes. Now if she could convince herself she was having a real date, everything would be perfect. She wished desperately she would have gone ahead and said yes to Arthur Little when he had asked her to Homecoming their senior year in high school, but it was such a pathetic invitation: "Neither of us have a date. Why don't we go together?" How could she have known that would be the first and last invitation she would ever get from someone of the male persuasion? If she had, she might have accepted if only to get the whole awkwardness of the experience under her belt. Who would open doors? Who would foot the bill? And, most stomach-clenching of all, what would happen at "Good night?"

And heaven forbid there would be a second or third date, then an actual relationship and further potential for—well—intimacy. Oh, how she wished she'd have taken care of these firsts before now. "Listen to me," she said to her reflection. She looked toward her bedroom window as if someone might be there spying on her, catching her in the act of daring to wish. "It's a free ticket to see Billy Ray Cyrus. By Monday, we'll be back to customer-mailman status. He's not any more interested in me than Arthur was."

"Yoo hoo, honey!" Sharon's voice sang through the screen door bringing Marilou back to herself, "Who's ready for a night on the town?"

Marilou gave herself one last look in the mirror and headed for the living room. She tried not to let Sharon's good looks dampen her bright mood. It was hard to deny though. Sharon was a fox. She had the guts to wear white rhinestone-studded suede with fringe hanging from the sleeves and pink cowboy boots. She really didn't have the legs for a mini-skirt, but Marilou had to admire her courage to put them out there, knock-knees and all.

"Don't you look sharp!" Sharon gestured for Marilou to turn in a circle. "Yes, yes. You made the right call on those boots. They're adorable!"

Before Marilou had a chance to return the compliment, a forest green Ford LTD pulled up to the curb. Ricardo opened the door almost before it came to a full stop. Marilou grabbed her purse. It didn't have anything in common with the rest of her outfit, but that couldn't be helped.

"Oooo, they're cute. Which one is mine?" Sharon asked over her shoulder, moving to the second step to make room for Marilou.

Marilou almost laughed at the question. The resemblance between the men was uncanny: small frames, neat mustaches, faces the shapes of hearts. What difference could it make to Sharon which one was "hers?"

As if they were engaged in some sort of gentleman one-upsmanship, the brothers greeted them, Ricardo with a polite bow of the head, Freddy with a kiss to the back of Sharon's hand. Ricardo took Marilou's arm as she descended the steps. Freddy ran ahead to open the car door.

Sharon slid into her seat. As Marilou settled in, she tried to shake the feeling she was in a play with the men following a script and just let herself enjoy the attention. It was finite after all.

Freddy looked in the rear view mirror. "Do you ladies like steak?"

Sharon raised her eyebrows at Marilou and mouthed the word, "Steak," fluffed her hair and slid all the way back in her deep seat. "We absolutely do like steak," she declared.

Sharon went on to fill the air with her melodic voice commenting on landmarks slipping past the windows. Marilou struggled to think of something interesting or witty to slide into the conversation, but by the time she thought of an anecdote, Sharon had already turned the conversation in a different direction, and Marilou's hard-sought story would no longer make any sense in context. She knew she should be grateful for Sharon filling the empty air in the car. Still, Marilou wished for an opportunity to shine just a little bit outside the shadow of her rhinestone-studded girlfriend.

Blandings' Steak House sat just before the state border, three miles from the exit for Rockford. It was known for having a pricey menu and a reservation list a mile long.

"Oh, we couldn't," slipped out of Marilou's mouth as Freddie pulled into the *Blandings'* parking lot.

Sharon shushed her. Freddy pulled into a slot and pushed the lever into Park.

"Nonsense. You have no idea what a treat it is for us to see Billy Ray. 'Cardo here is a bit of a Cyrus expert you might say."

Ricardo uttered three syllables that Marilou couldn't identify but recognized as a version of "Ah, go on," or "Oh, not me." She realized this was the first sound he had made since they'd pulled away from the curb.

Marilou was grateful they were seated at a large table rather than a cramped booth. She timed her sitting perfectly as Ricardo slid the chair under her thighs, just the right distance from the table. He wouldn't have to embarrass them both by struggling to push her any farther.

The meal followed like a symphony. They helped themselves to olives and raw vegetables from the lazy Susan relish tray, followed by salads made-to-order at their table. Marilou had never eaten in such a fancy restaurant, nor one that seemed to have been designed with her body in mind, from the size of the table to its distance from the others.

When Jake Blandings himself visited their table, shaking hands with Ricardo and slapping Freddy on the back, Marilou realized why the dining room was to her scale. Jake was the largest individual she had ever seen. His girth made Marilou feel almost petite.

"You've hardly touched your steak, Marilou. I hope nothing's wrong with it?" Jake looked genuinely concerned.

"Oh, no. It's delicious." Marilou wiped the corner of her mouth with her napkin. "To be honest," she thought of a reasonable explanation, "I'm just a little excited about the concert. Makes it hard to eat."

Jake relaxed. "Ah, well then. In that case, I'll have Meredith wrap it up nice for you. Best leftovers you'll ever eat." He shook hands with the brothers one more time and moved on to the next table.

As the waitress refilled their coffee cups, Sharon started in with trivia questions about Billy Ray. Marilou recognized the questions from Q106 and its Great Ticket Give Away that afternoon. But Sharon delivered them with such authority that anyone who didn't know better would have thought she was a Billy Ray aficionado. Ricardo found his tongue, beaming as he volleyed answer after answer at Sharon.

"I told you, 'Cardo knows his stuff." Freddy leaned toward Sharon. "Are you a big Billy Ray fan, too?"

"Oh, sure. Isn't everybody?"

Marilou couldn't help feeling that the men's chairs were drifting closer to Sharon's. *Believe in yourself and everyone else will do the same.*

Sharon held up her hands like she was trying to get their attention even though she already had it. "Okay, okay. What's Miley's real name and what's the name of her favorite doll?"

Ricardo narrowed his eyes, thinking.

Marilou said, "Destiny Hope."

Sharon's eyes widened. "Yes! And her doll?"

"Willie Nelson."

"Oh, my god." Sharon's voice sounded like a valley

girl. She looked from Ricardo to Freddy. "She's right. Miley walks around everywhere with a Willie Nelson doll!" She poked Ricardo in the shoulder. "Your girlfriend is brilliant!"

Marilou looked at her hands and started folding in each corner of her napkin, unable to bear seeing the expression that would be on Ricardo's face at the mention of the word, "girlfriend."

Instead of coughing or changing the subject, though, Ricardo said, "Yes. I believe she is."

Her hands stopped folding. Had she heard him correctly?

He turned his chair slightly toward her.

"How did you know that obscure piece of information about little Miley?"

Before she could say, Q106, Sharon bunched up her napkin, dropped it on the table, and looked at her watch.

"Come on, people. It's show time!"

The fans waiting to get into the concert looked like they had stepped right out of Country Music Television. They wore cowboy hats of all shapes and sizes and belt buckles that looked like they could have doubled as hubcaps.

"Have you ever seen so many mullets in all your life?" Sharon said this loudly enough that the mullet in front of them turned around and gave them a sneer from under his horseshoe mustache. Sharon didn't miss a beat. "No offense. I love a good mullet, if you've got the right hair for it, which you do—"

Marilou widened her eyes at Sharon, hoping she'd get the message: People can hear you!

Sharon pulled the tickets from her purse. "Fifth row. Front and center!" She fanned them out like a poker hand. "One for you. One for you."

As she handed each of them a ticket, the tick of the turnstiles caught Marilou's ear. Her stomach sank. She scanned the line of clicking gates for a way she could get in without having to squeeze through the tiny space. She felt an immediate need to pee.

A woman glided past her in a wheelchair. The ticket taker unhitched a velvet-covered rope and handed back her stub. Marilou exhaled. She would use that entrance and meet her friends on the other side. Not completely without embarrassment but a thousand times better than getting wedged between the flipping bars of the turnstile. She handed the man her ticket without making eye contact and joined the others.

"Who wants a beer?" Sharon said over her shoulder. "I'm buying." She stepped up to the counter before Ricardo and Freddy could reach for their wallets.

The beer threatened to roll over the sides of their cups, so they took their opening gulps before saying, "Cheers!" Marilou couldn't remember the last time she'd had a beer, and she certainly didn't remember it tasting as earthy and refreshing as it did right at this moment.

When they stepped through the entrance to their section, Marilou's breath caught in her chest. She had seen video of arenas and concerts, but she had never been in a space this big before.

Maybe it was the quick sips of beer on her near-empty stomach or the yellow tint of the lighting or the bassline of the music being piped over the PA, but Marilou felt dizzy and reached for the hand rail to catch her balance.

Ricardo touched her elbow. "Are you okay? You look pale."

She blinked. "No, I'm fine." It came out as a whisper. She cleared her throat and tried again. "I'm just happy to be here." She didn't care if she sounded like some country hick when she said it. "I've never seen anything like this. In person, I mean."

Ricardo touched her cheek. "Neither have I. Shall we sit?"

He led the group down the aisle toward Row E.

"Looks like this is it."

He stepped back so Marilou could go in first.

Thank goodness no one else was sitting in the row yet. She plopped herself into the padded folding chair. Ricardo kindly held his hands in his lap leaving her a little extra clearance on his side. She knew it was too much to hope that the seat next to her might be empty, but for now, she could be somewhat comfortable, even let her right knee wander a bit into the space of the empty seat next to her. At least until the person showed up.

It wasn't long before a trio took the vacant seats nearest her. The girls wore different versions of suede halter tops and pastel cowboy hats. From their glossy eyes and loud voices, Marilou concluded they had been drinking. How could they be old enough to drink? The girl next to her bumped Marilou's elbow, spilling the beer onto one of her new boots. Reflexively, Marilou apologized for the girl's carelessness, but the girl looked at her as if Marilou were an inconveniently placed armchair and turned back to her friends.

"Someone switch seats with me. I got the fat guy last time."

Marilou leaned forward hoping her body could absorb the embarrassing comment before it reached Ricardo's ears.

"It won't be too bad if you dab it away quickly." The sight of Ricardo's white handkerchief made Marilou want to cry. His finger brushed hers as she accepted it. Before she could thank him, the lights dimmed and an announcer's voice was introduced the opening act, The Bootery. Marilou didn't know any of their songs, but the girl next to her did and sang along with every word as she swayed in her seat.

Following two more sloshing incidents, Marilou decided to cut her losses and finish off her beer. It helped her stomach feel less empty and took some of the sting out of the girl's comment. She dropped her empty cup on the floor and pushed it under her chair with the heel of her boot.

Ricardo handed her a full one. "Sharon bought us another."

Down the row, Sharon held up her cup and mouthed, "Cheers!"

Marilou leaned in close to Ricardo's ear. "I hope you don't think we always drink like this."

He smiled back and clinked her cup with his own.

As The Bootery announced their final song, Marilou regretted all the water and coffee at dinner. And the beer. The more she tried not to think about it, the more she simply *had* to go. Right now.

Marilou grabbed her purse and made her way down the row. Over Ricardo. Over Freddy. Over Sharon. The two people on the end saw her coming and were kind enough to step into the aisle so she could get through. She started to walk toward the exit as rapidly as her full bladder would let her, only to find a line snaking from the ladies' room. She took her place and shifted her weight slowly from foot to foot, trying to focus on keeping the pee in and the memories of halter top girl out, willing the women ahead of her to hurry it up. She clenched her jaw and started to sweat. Ordinarily, she'd have waited for the handicapped stall so she'd have more room, but she was desperate.

There.

She tried to glide as smoothly as she could to the stall that had just opened, but, before she could even get the door to latch, her bladder let go sending a trickle of warmth down her right leg into her boot. Frantically, she pulled up her skirt and sat on the toilet, peed right through her underwear and stayed there on the bowl, frozen—while toilets flushed, faucets whooshed, hand dryers blew. She knew she was preventing someone else from relieving herself, and she didn't care. Maybe halter top girl was next in line, doing her own version of the potty dance. Marilou smiled at the thought.

She sat.

She sat until the last footsteps clicked out on the tile. She pictured Ricardo in his seat next to her empty one, Sharon torn between staying to see Billy Ray and coming to check on her. Marilou tried to think of how she could explain what had taken her so long.

The crowd roared, and she could make out the first notes of "Some Gave All."

No, she would escape. Apologize later. How much would it cost to take a cab back into Wisconsin? Probably more than the twenty bucks she had in her wallet. She balanced her purse on her knees and fished inside. Her hand landed on the letter from Social Security. She had told herself she wouldn't open it until the morning after her date, but she saw no reason to prolong the agony now.

She read the first sentence. *We are writing to notify you that your application to receive Disability Benefits has been denied.* Denied. She read on to learn that the measure of her "Residual Function Capacity" indicated a number of work situations that would make her employable. As such, she was unqualified to receive benefits. She thought of Jake Blandings working as the head chef in a bustling supper club. She thought of her able-bodied father and his threats to go on welfare. She almost laughed and wished he were alive, so she could call him up and tell him he never would have qualified. Denied.

The crowd roared again.

She thought of Ricardo, who had been nothing but kind since the moment she offered him that first chocolate. Her first concert, her first date, and here she was in wet underwear feeling sorry for herself. She took a deep breath. She'd come farther than she ever thought she could and wasn't about to let it slip away now. "When you've got nothing to lose, you've got nothing to lose." She'd said it out loud, her echo telling her again, "Nothing to lose."

Marilou stood up, checked her skirt for spots, tucked its hem into her waistband and hooked her thumbs into the elastic of her underwear. Balancing herself against the stall wall, she wrestled first one leg hole, then the other over her boots. She crumpled the panties into a ball and shoved them into the sanitary napkin receptacle next to the toilet paper. Let someone else worry about them when she was long, long gone from this place. She dabbed herself off best she could with toilet paper and let her skirt fall loose. Not caring whether someone walked in, she let herself out of the stall and leaned on the sink while she removed her boot and dabbed it off with Ricardo's handkerchief. The boot wasn't as wet as she'd thought it would be. She punched the button on the hand dryer and held the boot there for three cycles until it was dry enough to put back on her foot.

As she left the restroom, she felt a little breeze under her skirt with each step, pleasantly surprised with the sensation. She'd never gone without underwear and had to admit the freedom of it felt good. Darned good. Each step reminded her of her new mantra, which she shortened to "Nothing to lose."

Screw the girl in the halter top. Marilou had as much right to take up space as the girl did, with her swishing hair and gyrating hips. Marilou stepped up to the concession stand and ordered four beers, with a cardboard carrier, please, and not so full this time. She'd find her way back to her seat and tell the others a long beer line had held her up.

She would enjoy her first concert and maybe even get her first kiss.

Acknowledgments

The stories in this collection hold the touches of many hands. I will be forever grateful to: my husband, Rob, whose default answer is "Sounds like a great idea," and whose confidence in me has always exceeded my own. Quite simply, his loving support (and sharp editor's eye) made this book possible; my children, Shelby and Ethan, whose creative sparks are inspiring and contagious; and my mom, Cathy Hlavacek, who has always believed in me. Without. Fail. Period.

Some of these stories were workshopped under the keen-eyed mentorship of Judy Bridges at Redbird Studio and with the help of the dedicated and generous writers "at the table" more than a few years ago. Other stories were made better under the mentorship of Sandra Scofield, Steven Huff, and Randall Keenan, and at the workshop tables of Sterling Watson, Venise Berry, and Jedediah Berry in the Solstice MFA program directed by Meg Kearney. My "Solstice Siblings" provided valuable feedback: the perfect mix of challenge and encouragement.

In addition, I thank the members of the Red Oak Writing Roundtables, whose dogged determination and trust have made my own writing better. I'd start naming names but would surely leave someone out. You know who you are.

Finally, I am eternally grateful to the staff at Cornerstone Press under the direction of Dr. Ross Tangedal. Their enthusiasm and professionalism made this a book of which I am so very proud. Not only do they make me optimistic about the future of the publishing world but of the world in general.

Thank you.